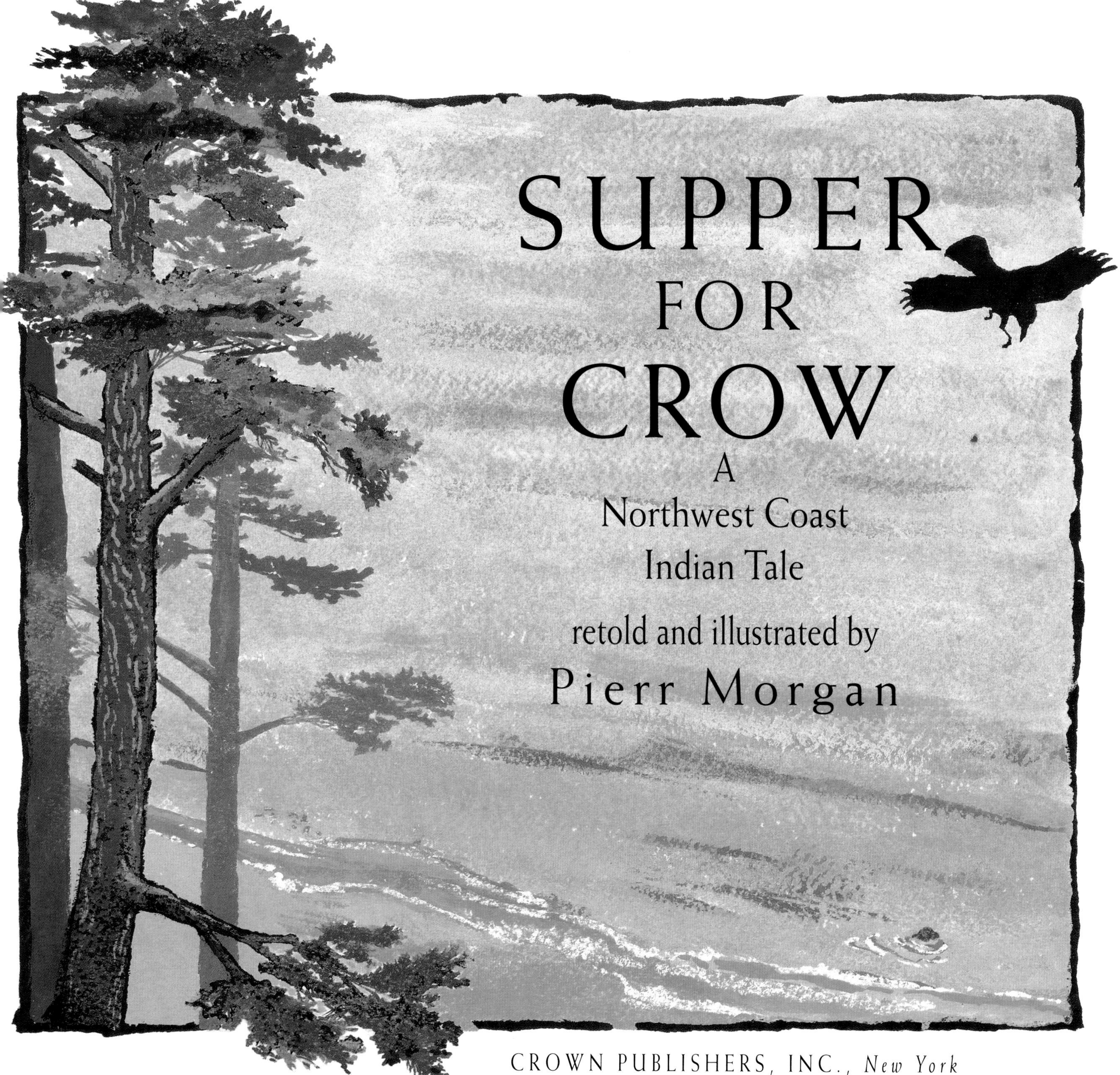

SUPPER FOR CROW

A Northwest Coast Indian Tale

retold and illustrated by
Pierr Morgan

CROWN PUBLISHERS, INC., *New York*

For my son, Aaron, his dad, Steve Leitz, and for Isabelle
with love — Pierr (T'idi·ĕuk)

Published by Crown Publishers, Inc., a Random House company,
201 East 50th Street, New York, NY 10022
CROWN is a trademark of Crown Publishers, Inc.
Manufactured in Singapore

Library of Congress Cataloging-in-Publication Data
Morgan, Pierr.
Supper for Crow : a Northwest Coast Indian tale / by Pierr Morgan.
p. cm.
Summary: Mama Crow and her hungry babies learn an important lesson in
greed and gullibility from Mischievous Raven.
1. Indians of North America—Northwest Coast of North America—Legends.
2. Raven (Legendary character)—Legends.
[1. Indians of North America—Northwest Coast of North America—Legends.
2. Raven (Legendary character)] I. Title.
E78.N78M66 1995
398.24'528864—dc20   93-41665

ISBN 0-517-59378-5 (trade)
0-517-59379-3 (lib. bdg.)

10 9 8 7 6 5 4 3 2 1

First Edition

This illustrations in this book were done in Winsor & Newton gouache and
Higgins black ink on 140-lb. Arches watercolor block.

AUTHOR'S NOTE

Some time ago I lived on the Makah (muh-KAH) Indian Reservation in Neah Bay, Washington, where I enjoyed the Pacific Ocean as my front yard and Isabelle Ides, a Makah elder and basket maker, as my next-door neighbor.

One rainy afternoon we were weaving baskets by her wood stove, listening to the ocean and the noisy crows outside while our fingers twirled and twisted cedar bark and bear grass, when Isabelle looked up from her basket and said, "I'm gonna tell you a story." Oh MY, did she tell me a story. And when she was done, she just grinned at me and kept weaving and chuckling, weaving and chuckling.

Isabelle told me this one story about Crow and Raven, but the Northwest Coast Indians have many stories about Raven. Although he is usually up to mischief, his greed has often brought good fortune to mankind, as told in the Creation myths. His skills as a trickster—like those of his Southwest cousin, Coyote—inadvertently make him one of life's great teachers. Even Mama Crow, who still gets tricked now and then when she isn't paying attention, knows that no amount of talk can make up for a good jolt of firsthand experience.

In this retelling, I've tried to retain the flavor of Isabelle Ides's language. Like most Native American tales, this story has been passed down by word of mouth from generation to generation. When Isabelle was a little girl, a Makah elder told children this story and many others. They served as both entertainment and as an introduction to cultural values, delivering a message without moralizing.

Because it was Isabelle who passed this story on to me, I decided to set the tale in 1899, the year of her birth, and place it where she grew up, on the northwest coast of Washington. In the background of the paintings, boatloads of neighboring Indians gather for a potlatch—or "giveaway" celebration—serving as a contrast to the greediness of Raven and the baby crows, and displaying the generosity that *Supper for Crow* teaches us to appreciate. Whenever the Makah see someone taking more than his or her share, they give a knowing nod and say, Clo͞ok-SHO͞OD—Raven!

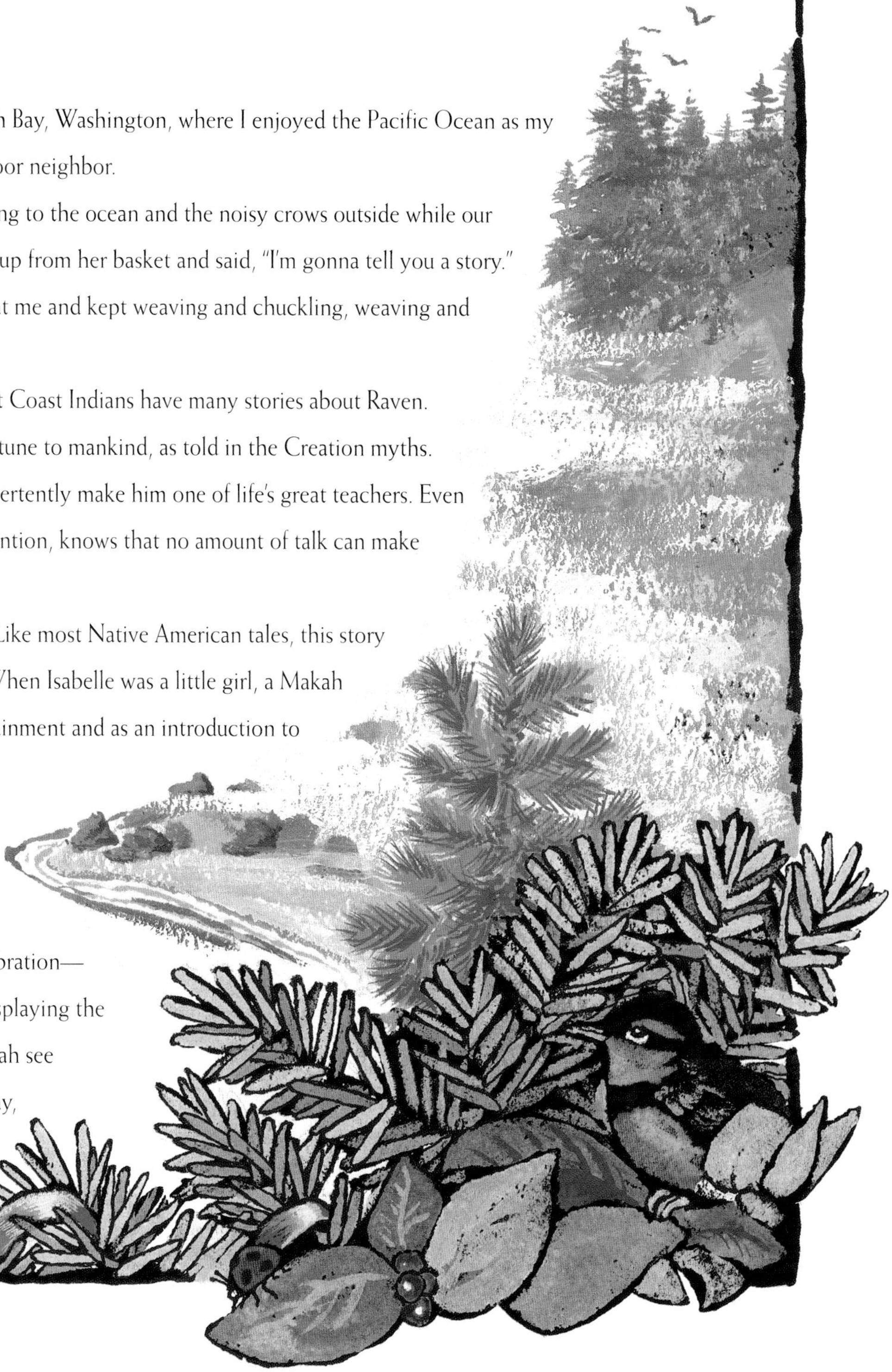

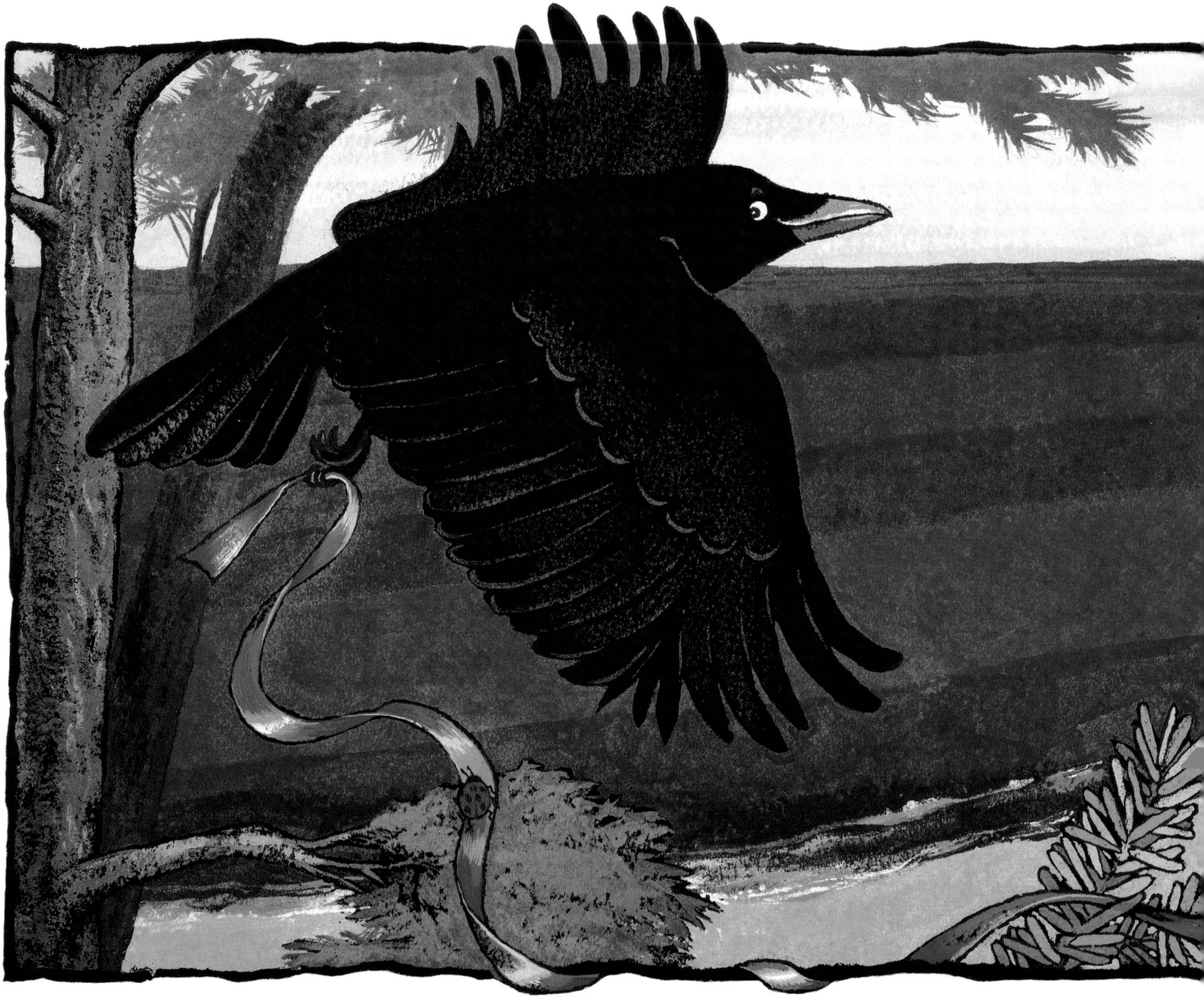

This is a story about Crow

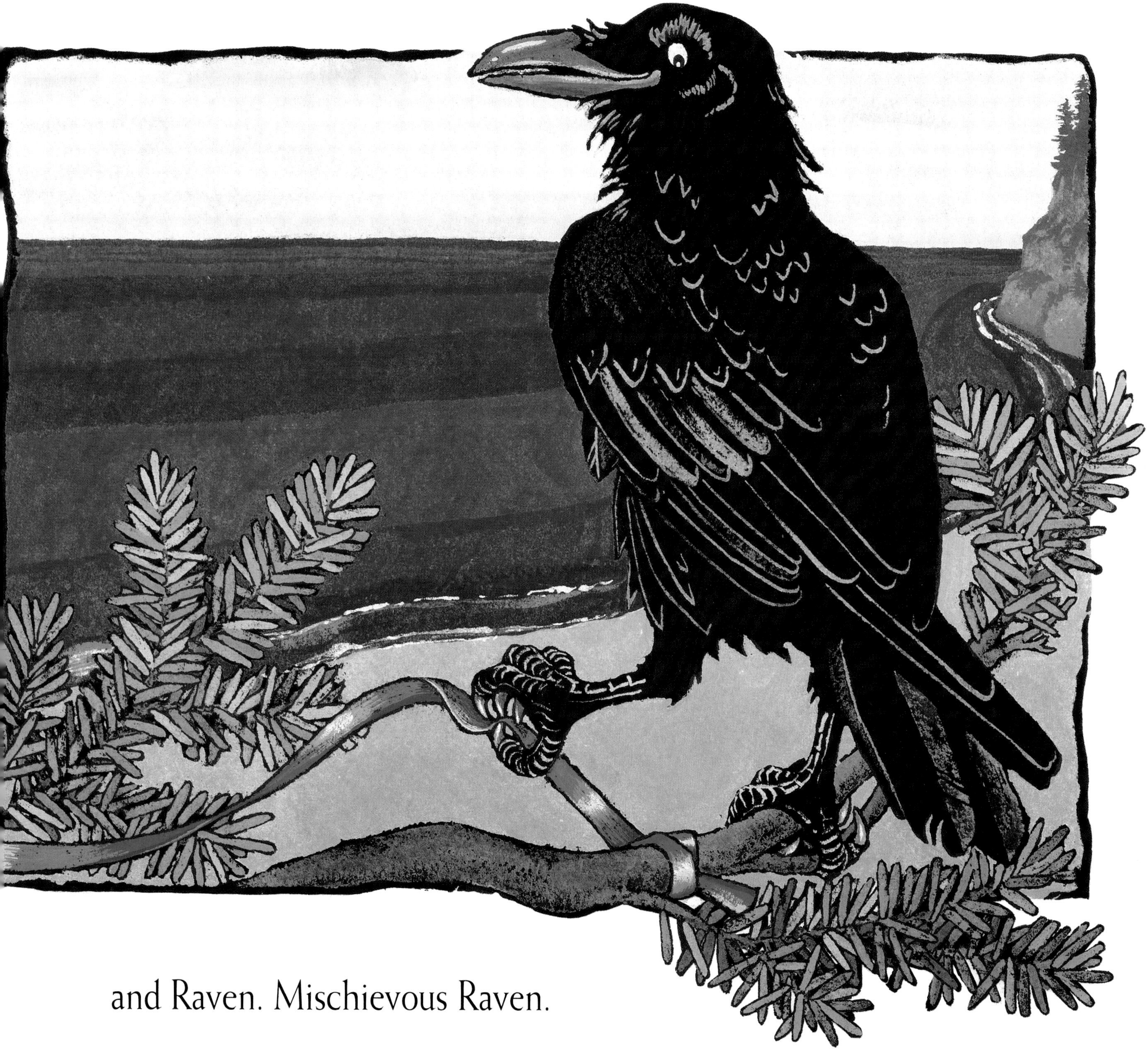

and Raven. Mischievous Raven.

Now, Crow had many babies. Oh MY, Mama Crow had many babies. And they were *hungry*. Mama Crow looked in her cupboard, but there was nothing in it.

"Mama, we are hungry!" the baby crows said.

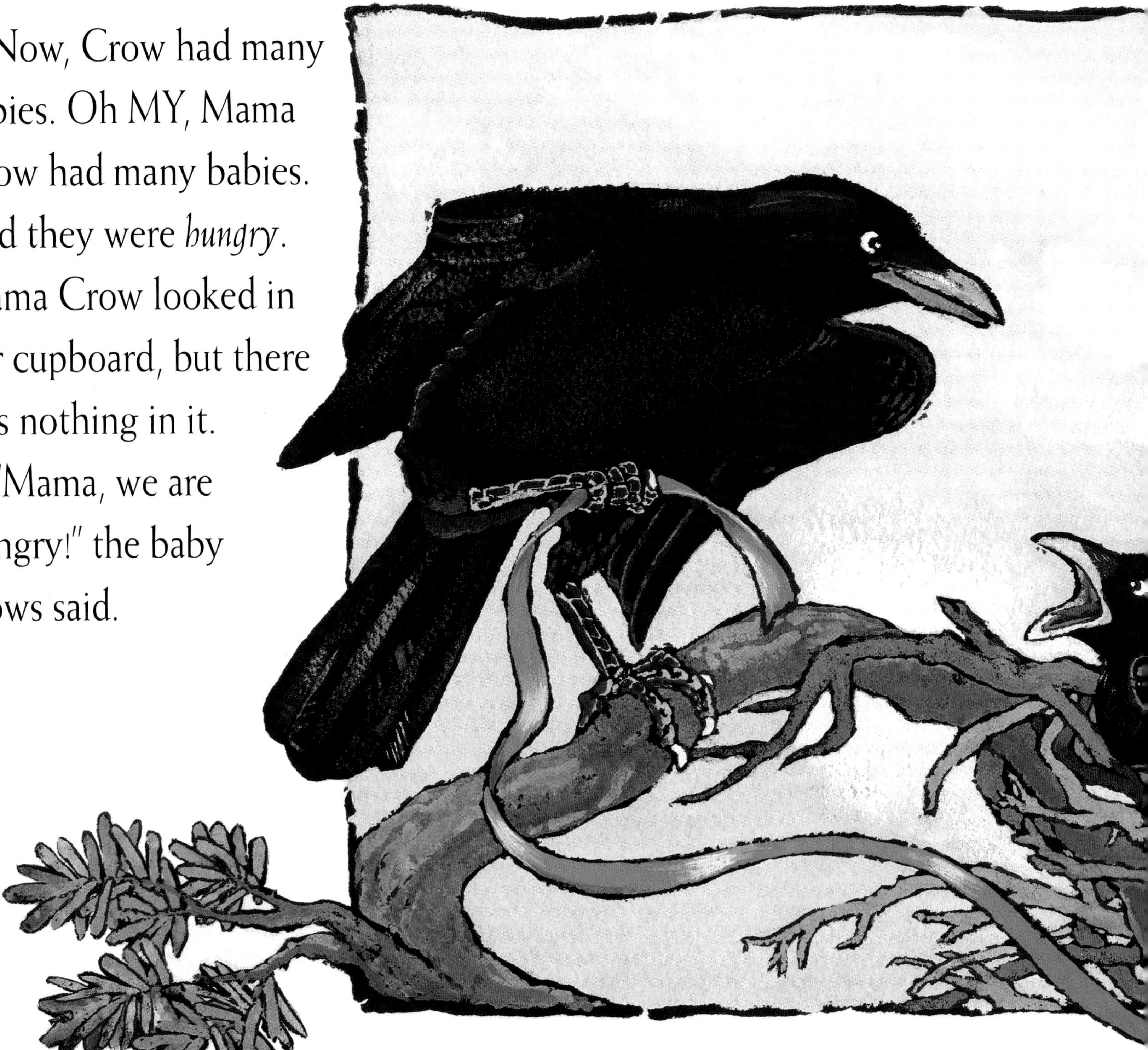

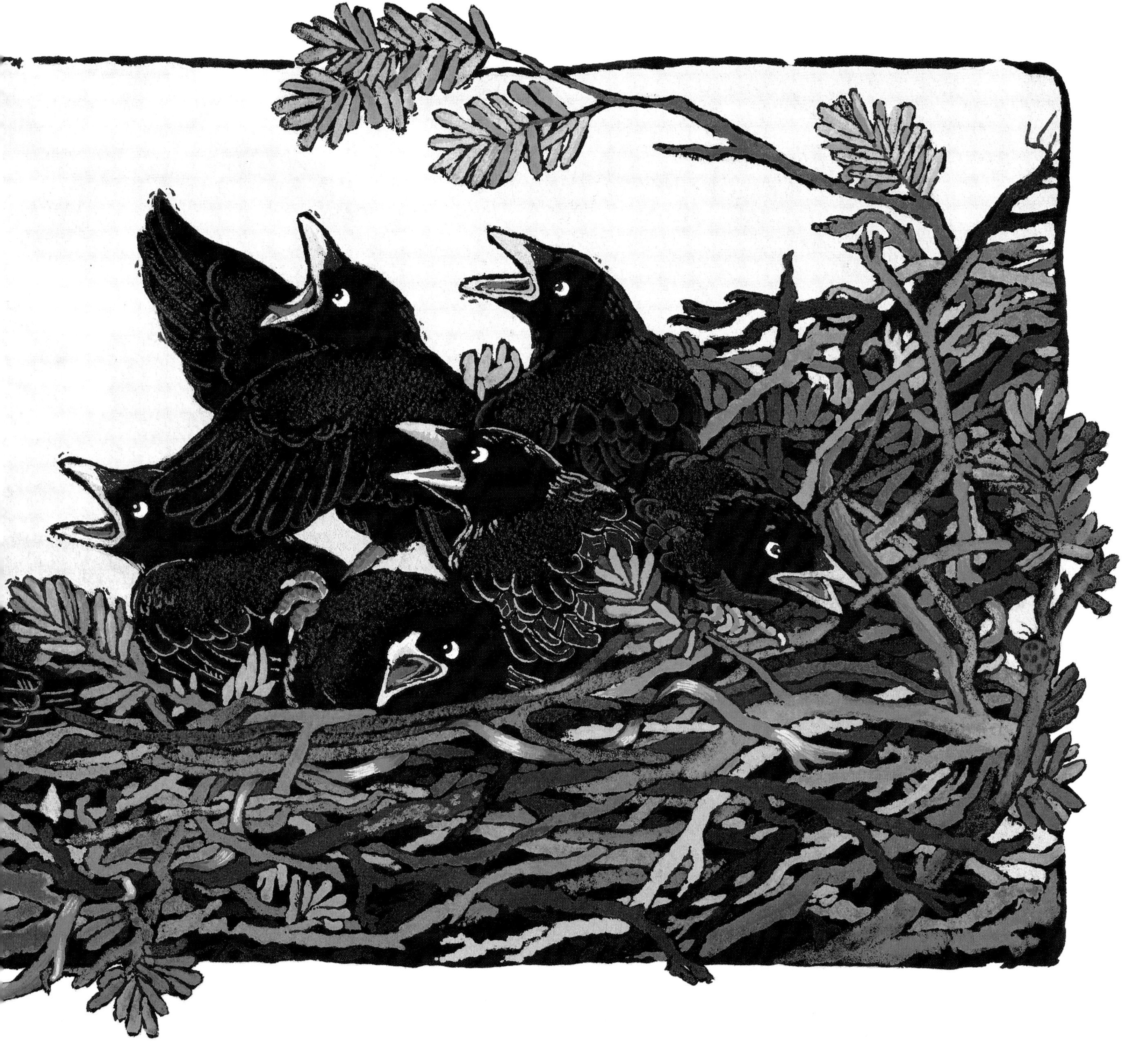

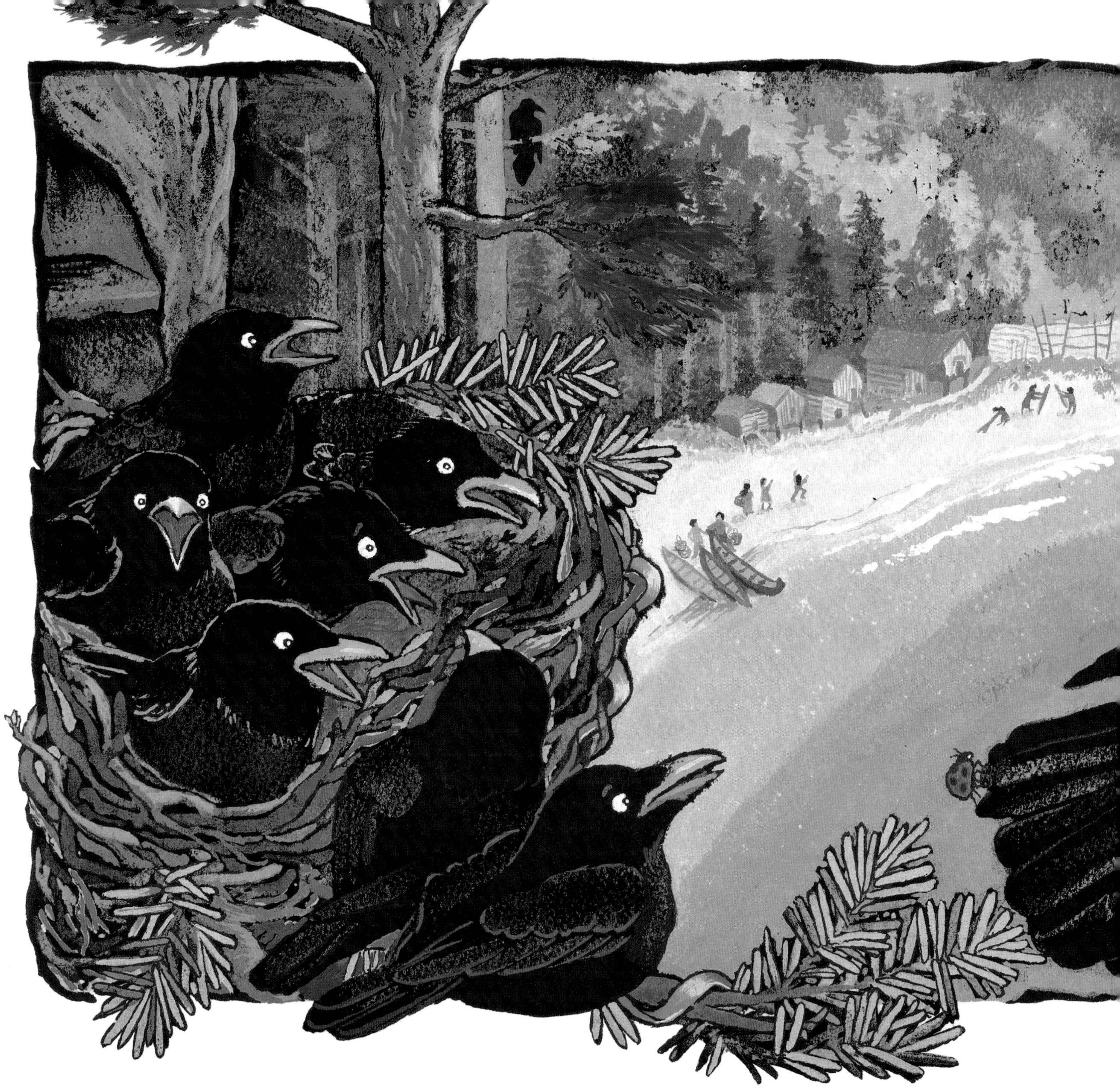

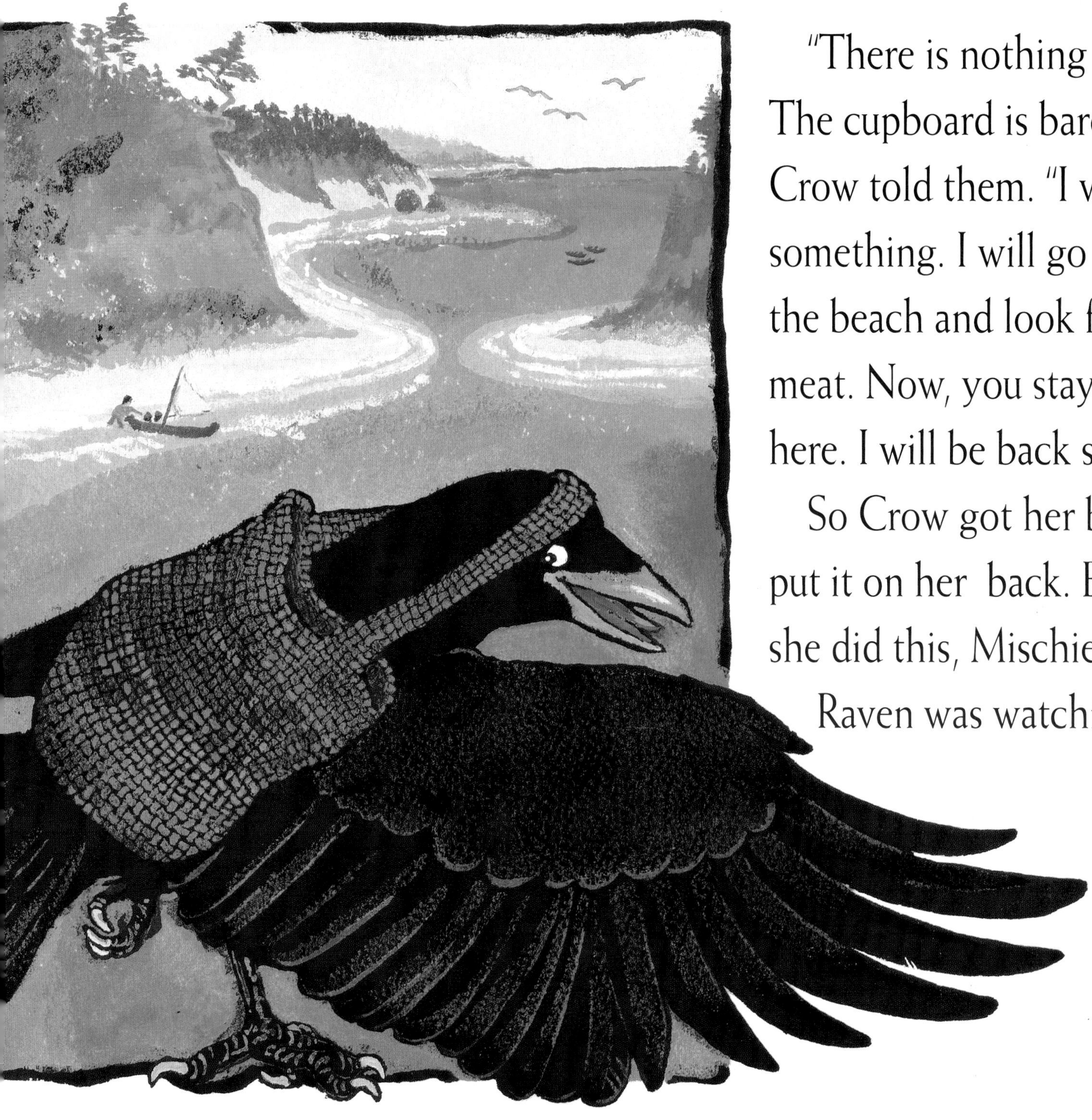

"There is nothing to eat. The cupboard is bare," Mama Crow told them. "I will find something. I will go down on the beach and look for seal meat. Now, you stay right here. I will be back soon."

So Crow got her basket and put it on her back. But while she did this, Mischievous Raven was watching her.

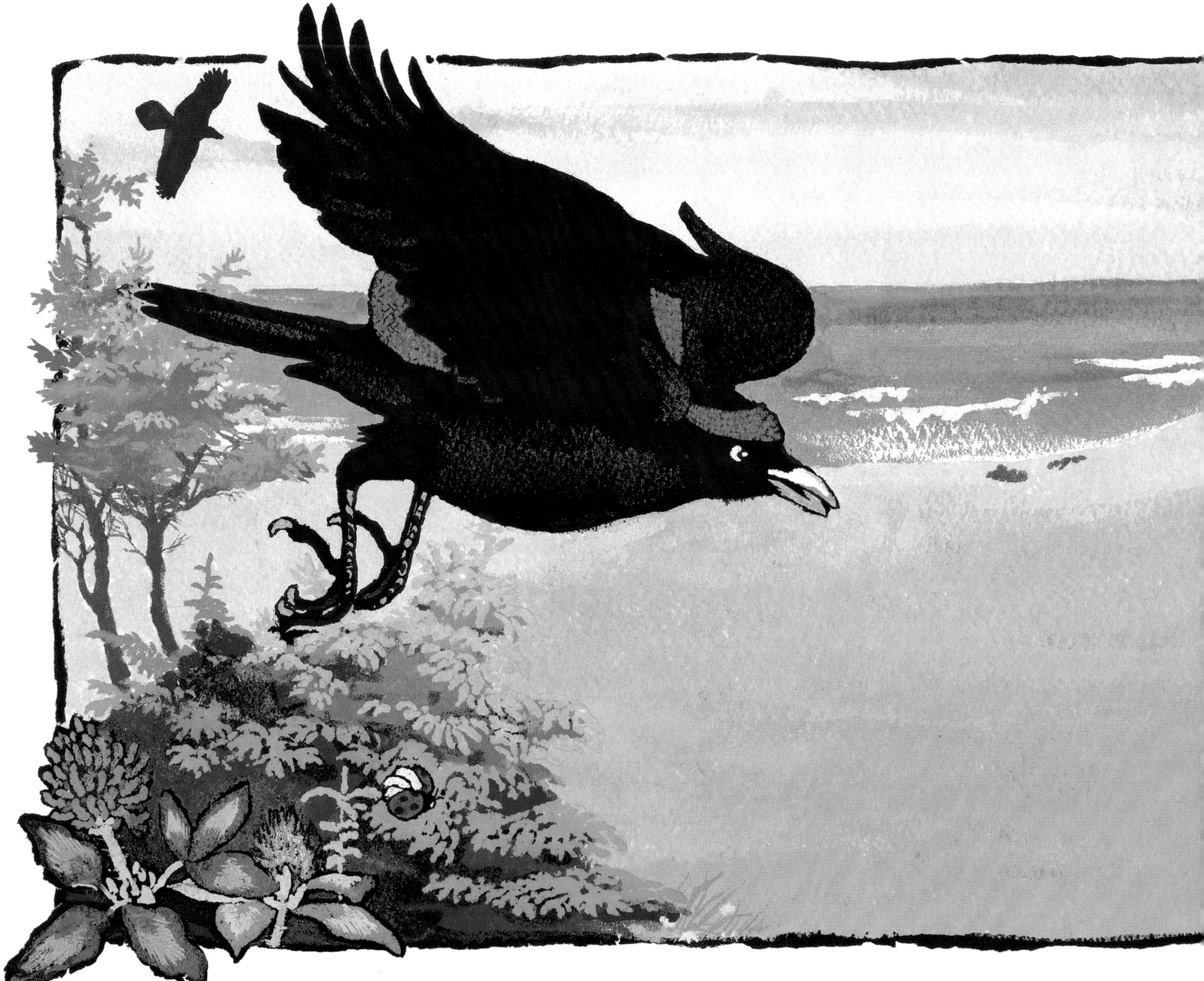

Crow started down the beach. She sang a song as she went.

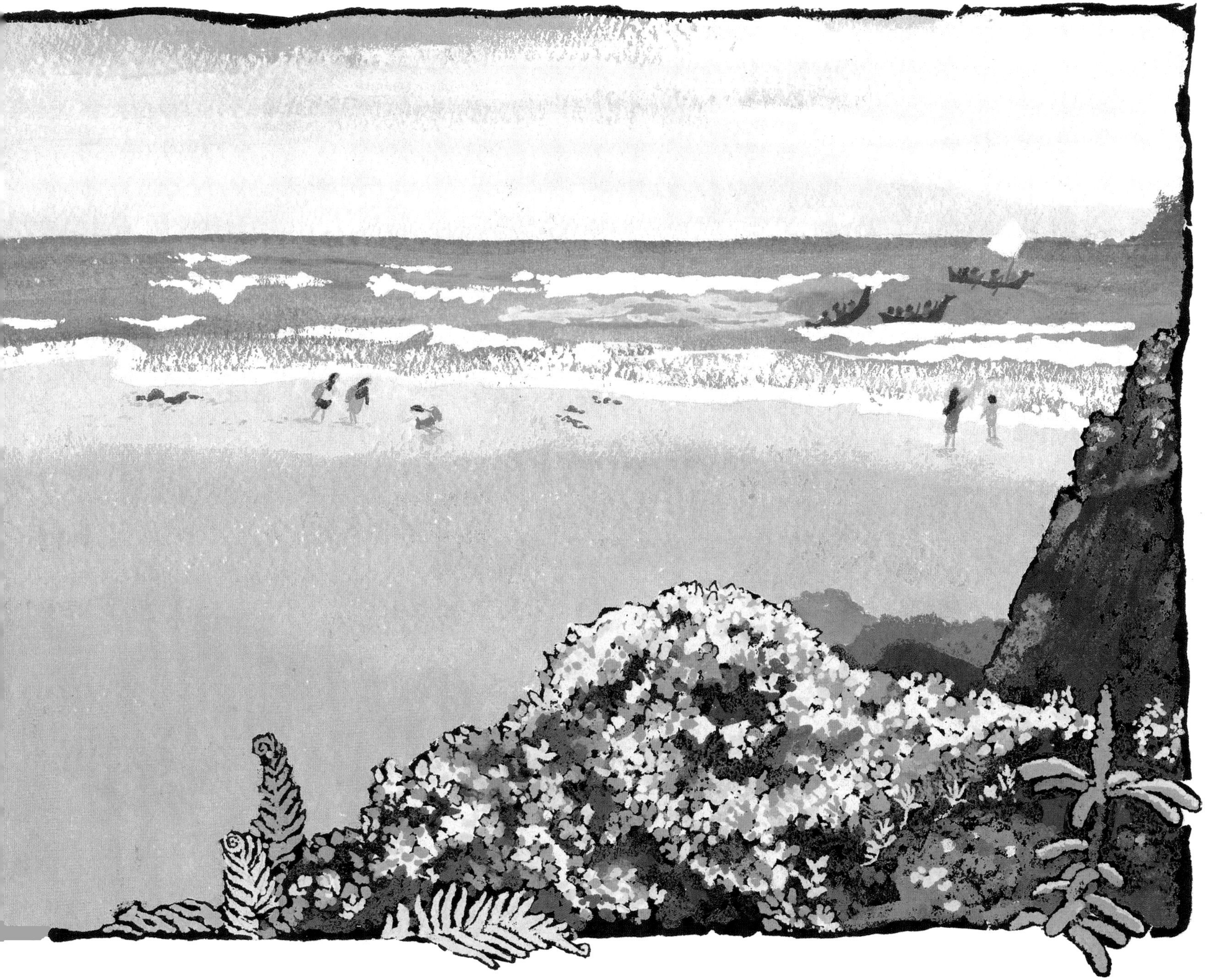

"I am hunting for seal meat, I am hunting for seal meat," she sang.

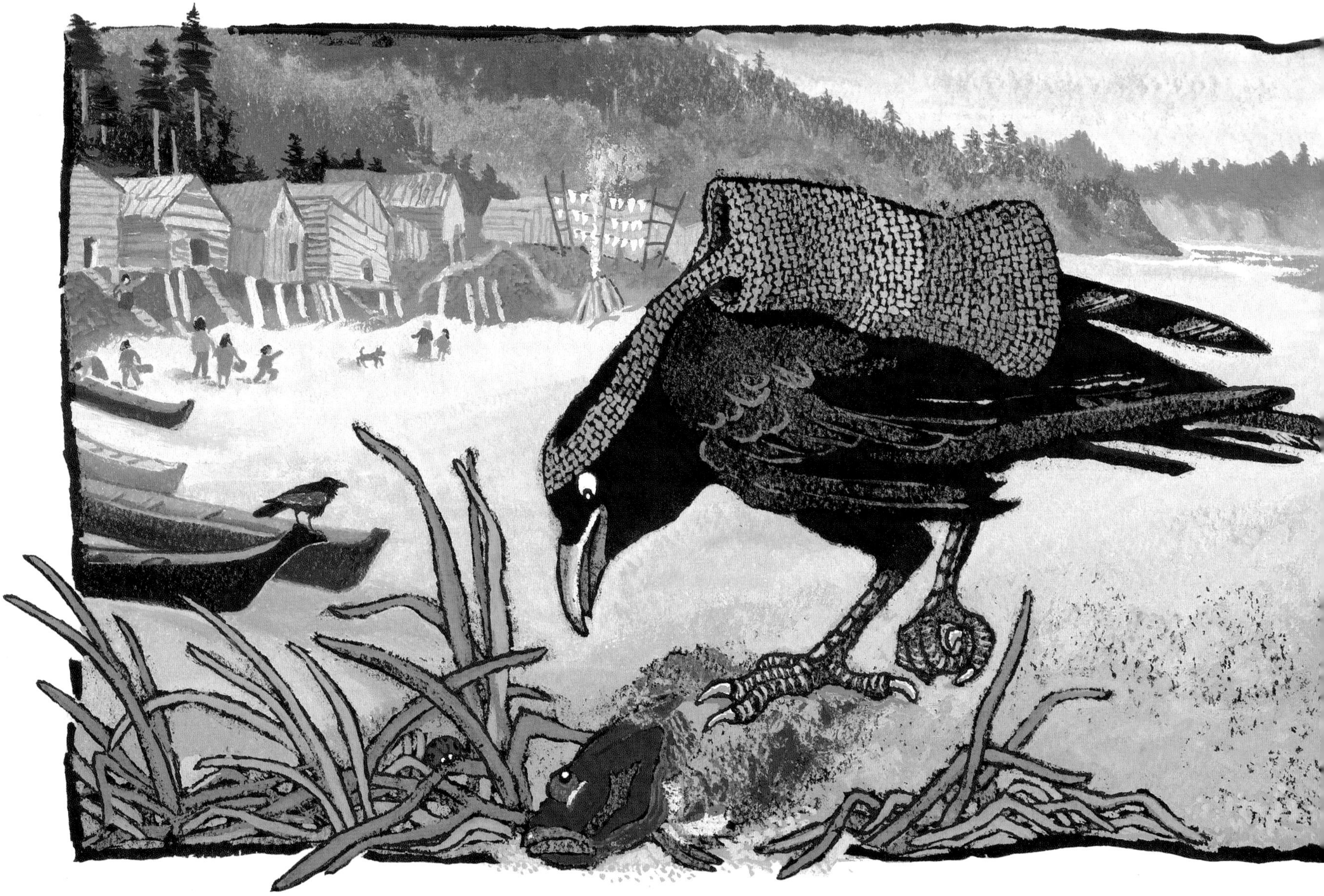

Then Crow saw something dark in the sand. She looked closer.

"Oh, it's just a bullhead," Mama Crow said.

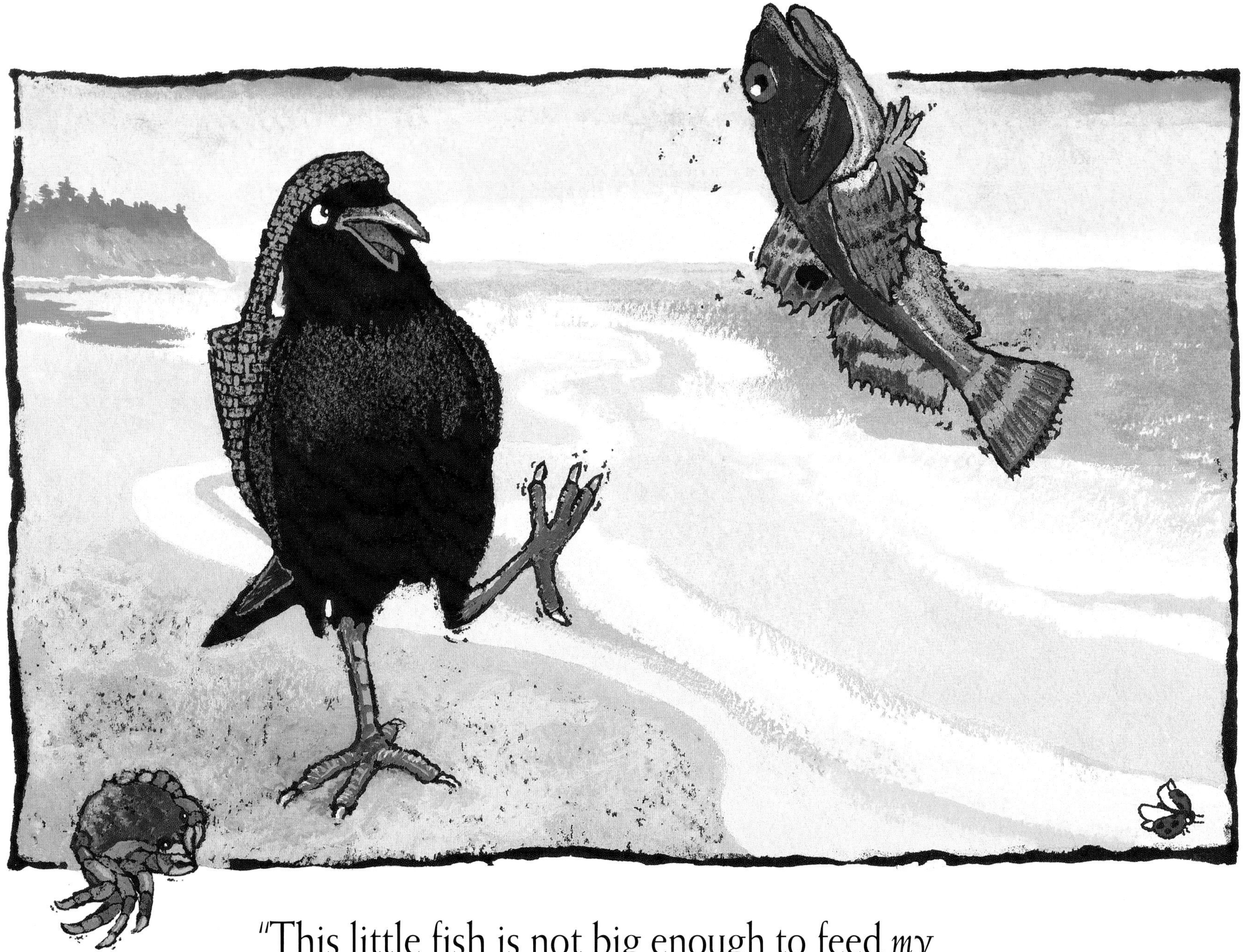

"This little fish is not big enough to feed *my* hungry children." And she gave it a kick and kept walking and singing, walking and singing.

Then she found some seal meat. Oh, how happy she was. MY, Crow was happy!

"How happy my children will be when I bring this seal meat home," said Mama Crow.

Then Crow heard Raven's voice behind her.

"Let me put that seal meat in your basket for you, Crow," said Mischievous Raven. "It looks so heavy."

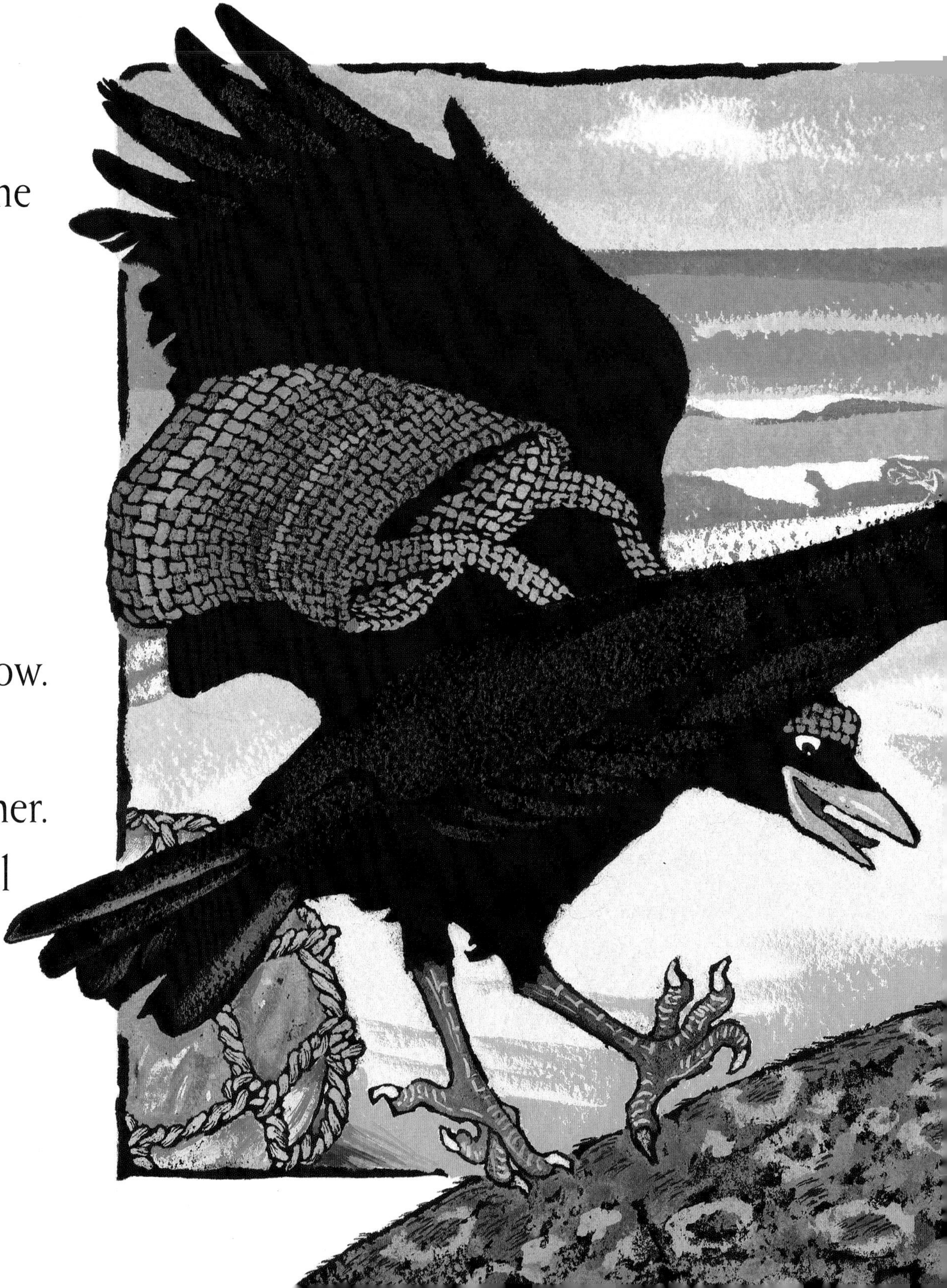

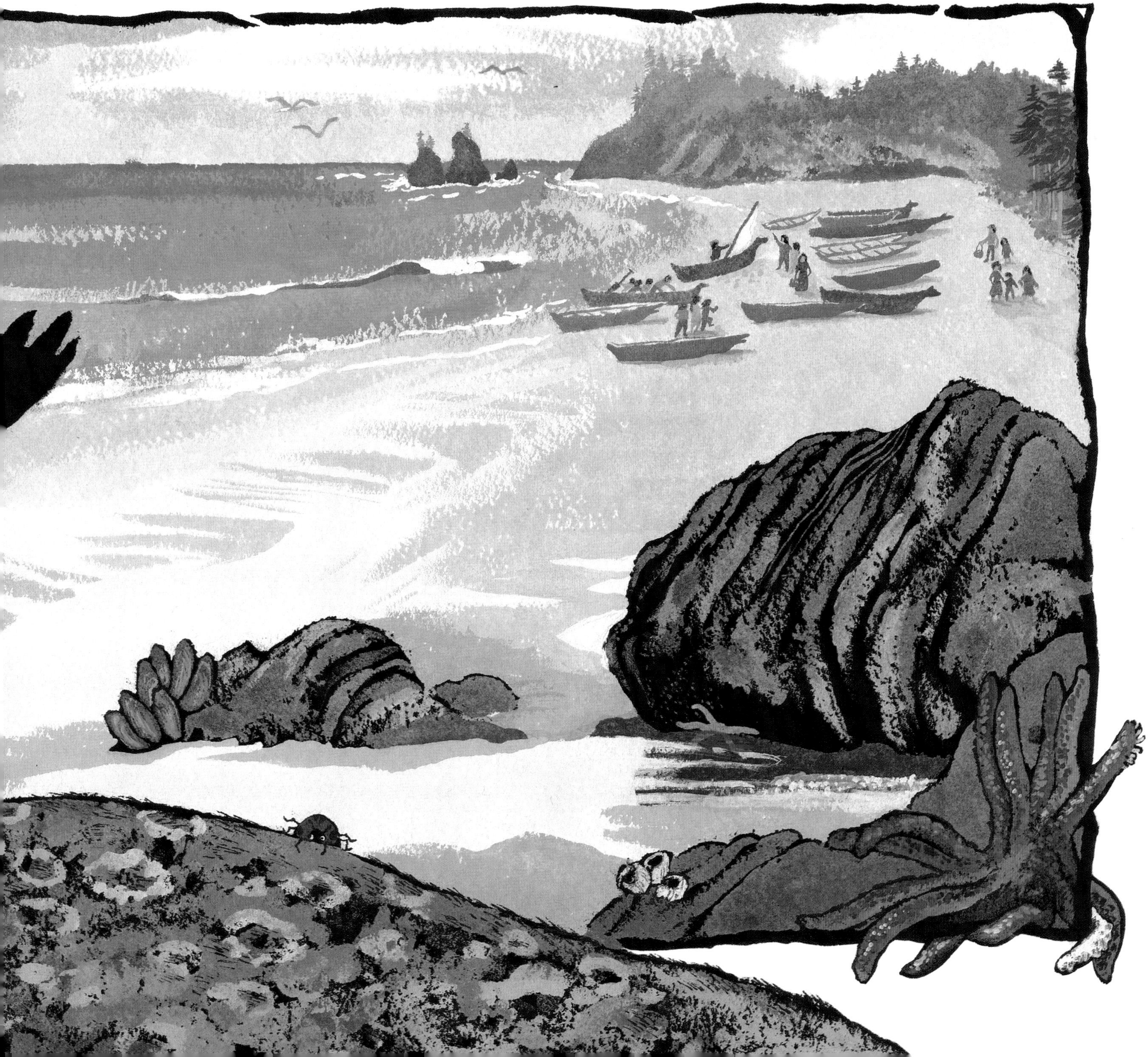

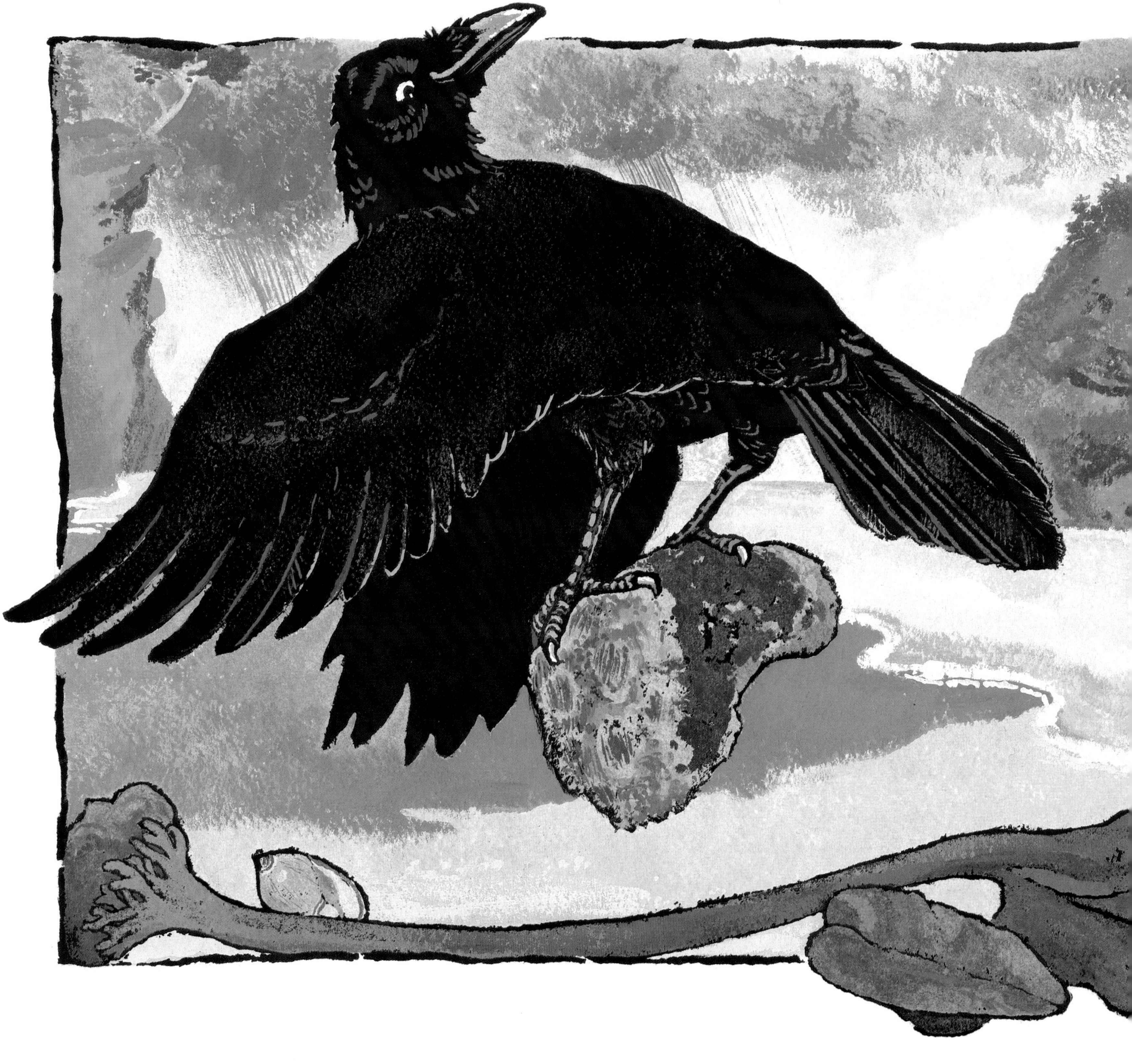

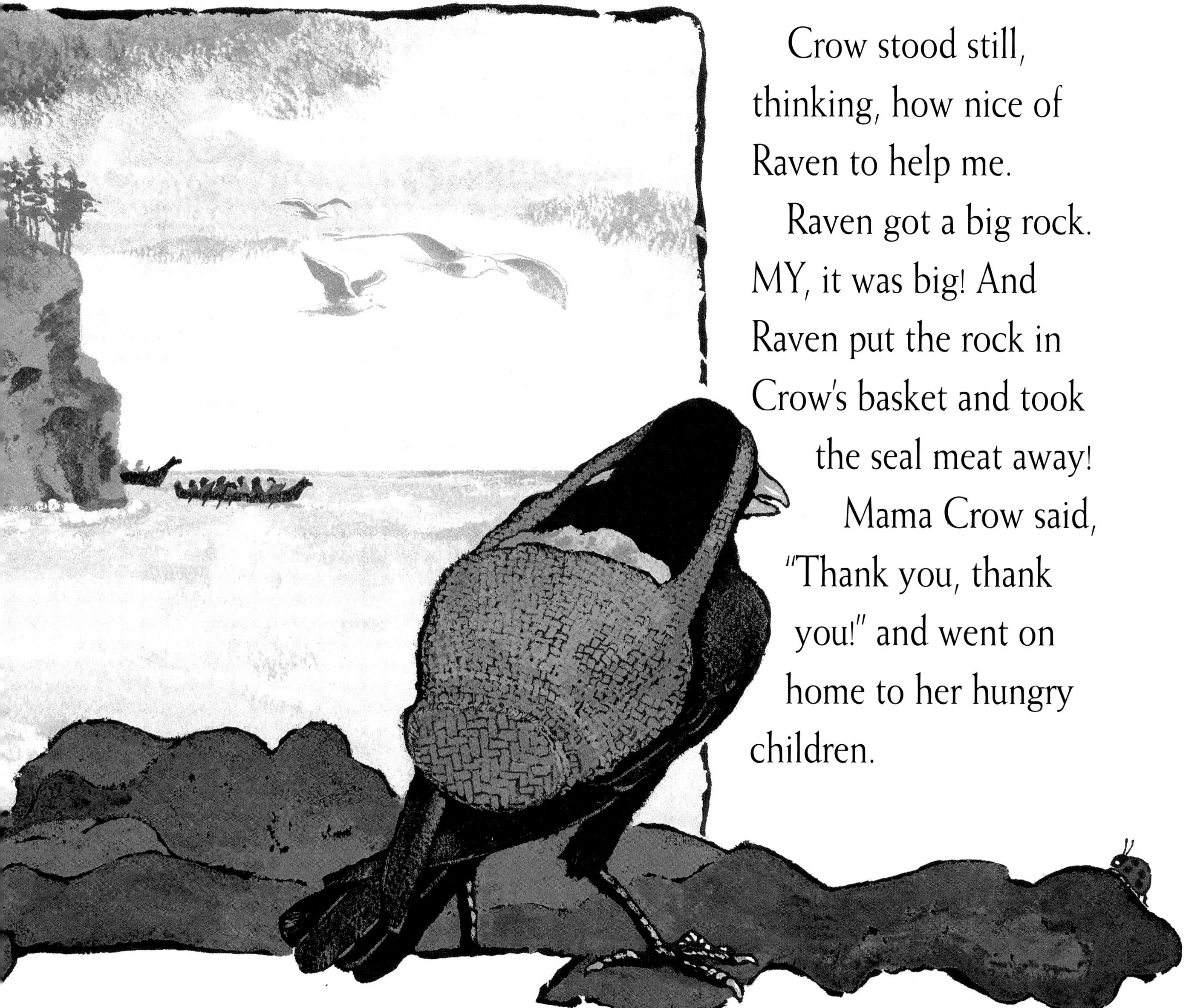

Crow stood still, thinking, how nice of Raven to help me.

Raven got a big rock. MY, it was big! And Raven put the rock in Crow's basket and took the seal meat away!

Mama Crow said, "Thank you, thank you!" and went on home to her hungry children.

When Crow got home, she said, "Get the biggest platter we have!"

Her children ran and got a big platter. MY, it was big. They put it on the floor.

Then Mama Crow took her basket and emptied it onto the platter.

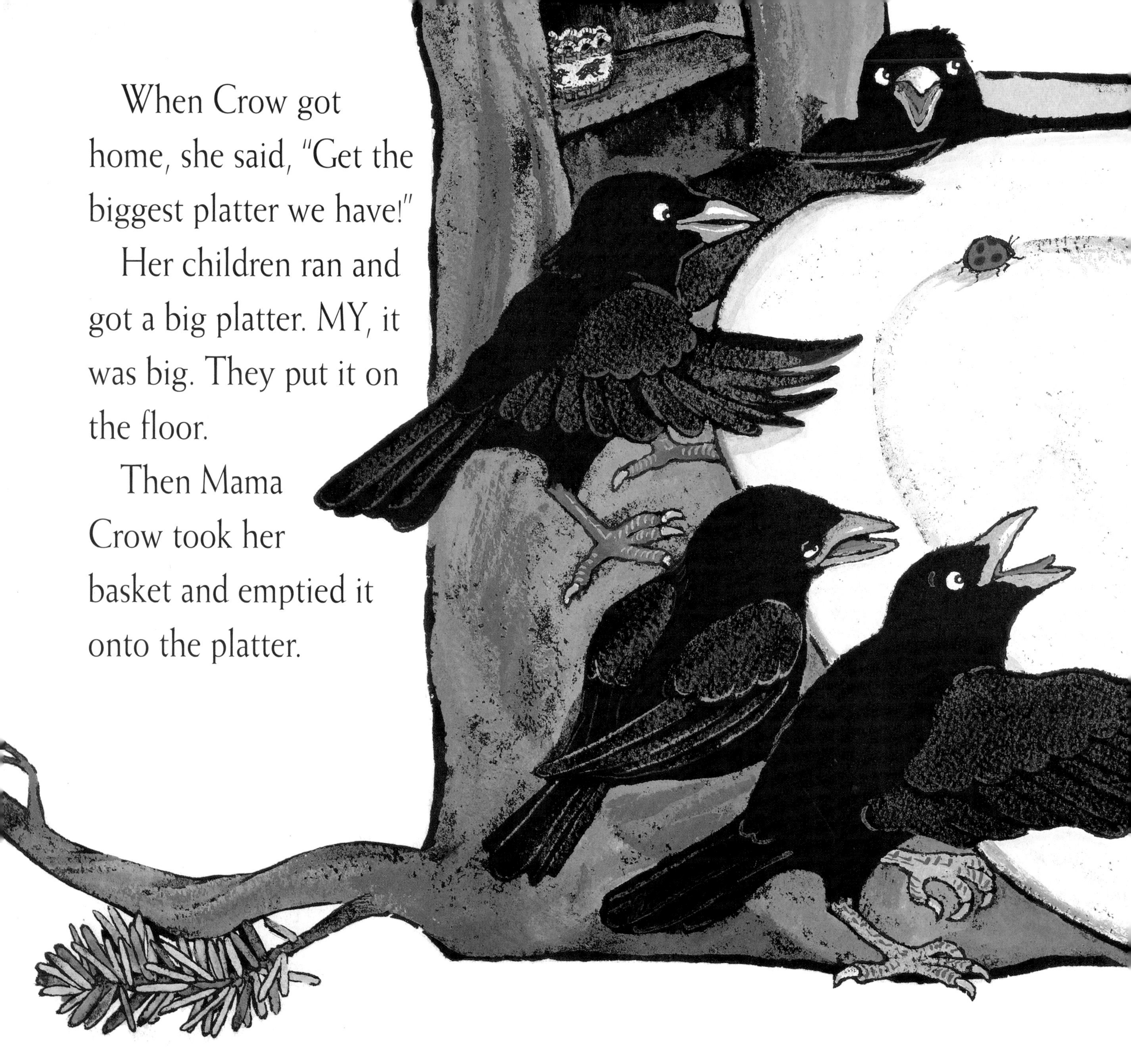

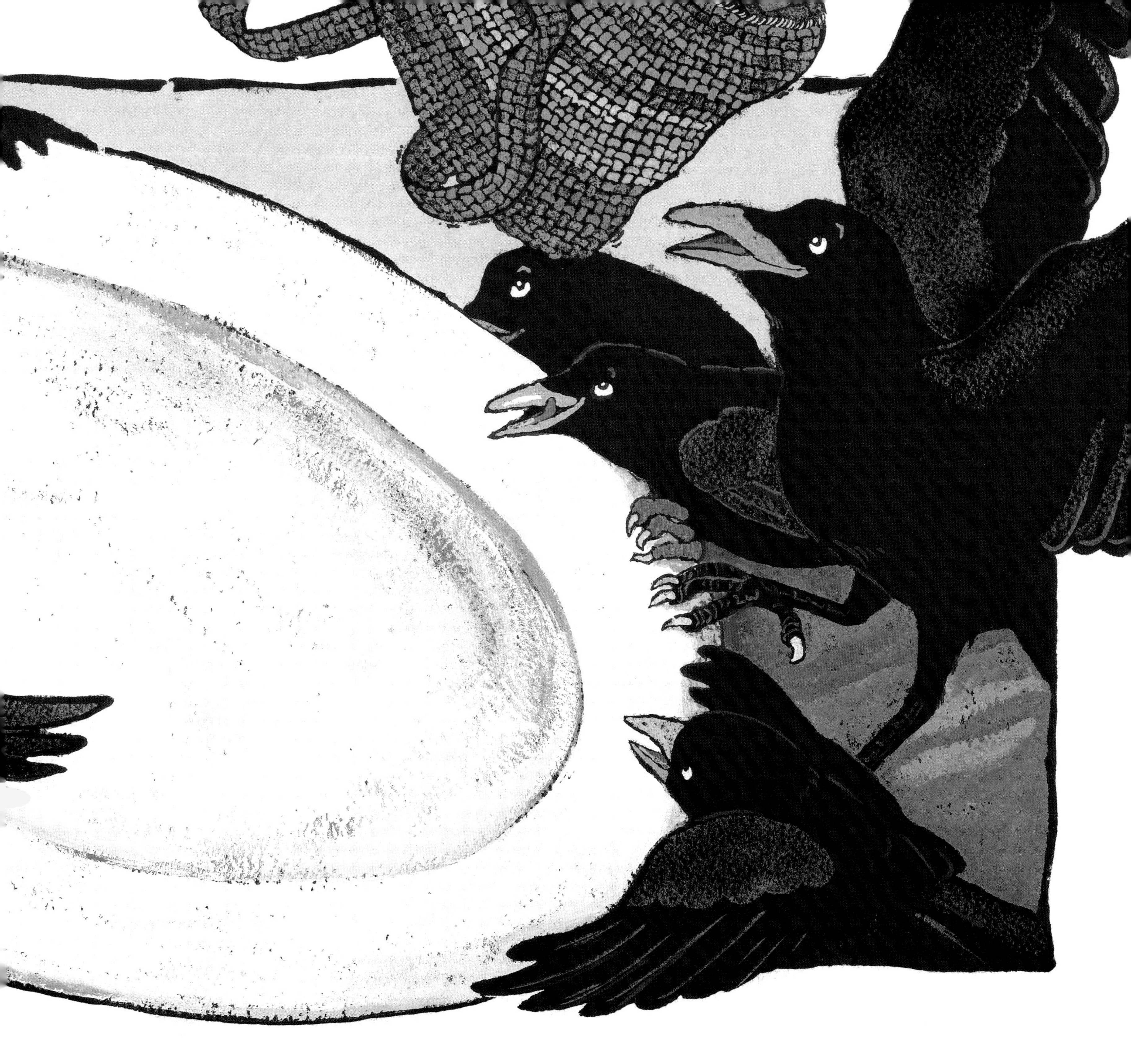

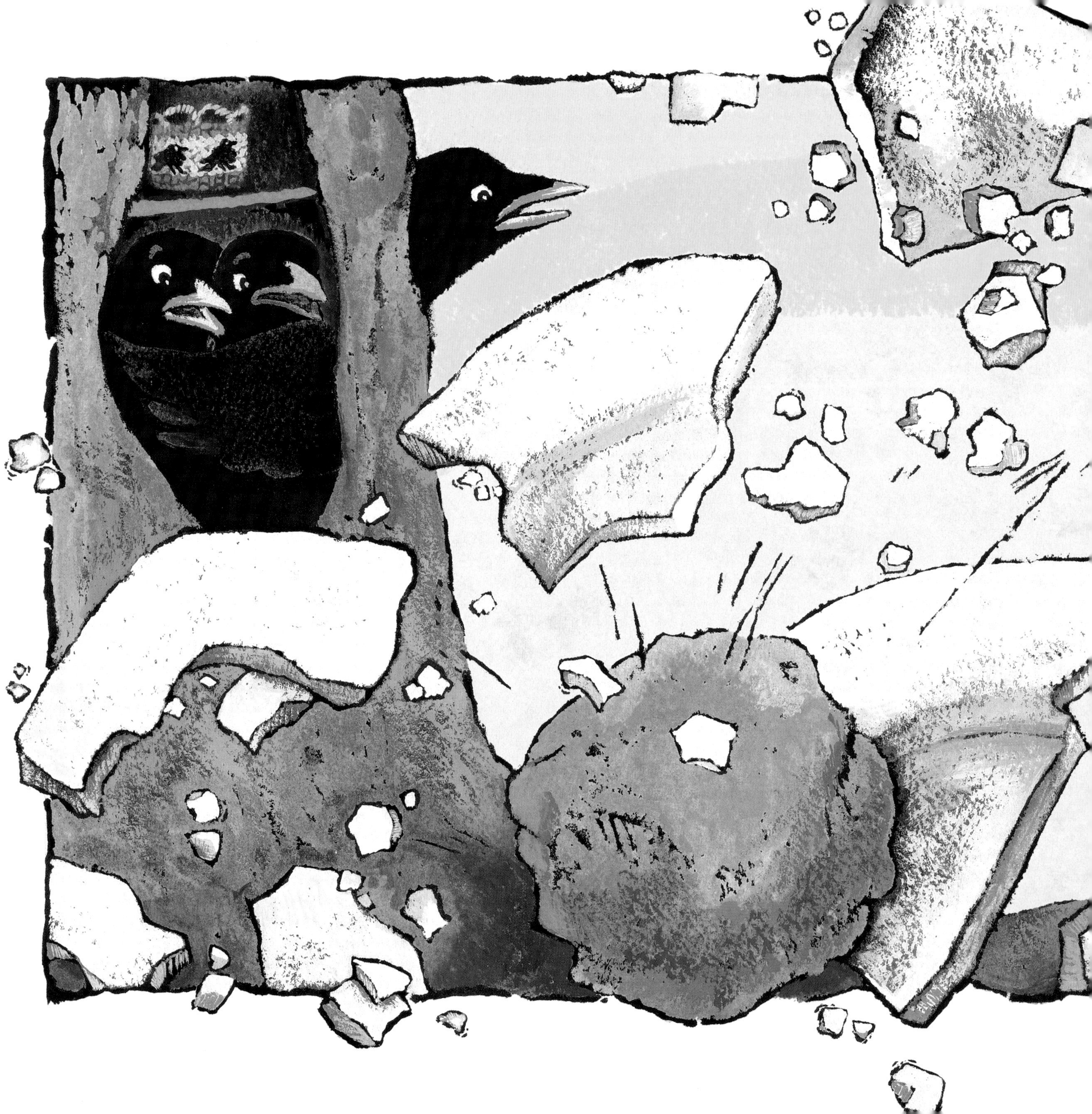

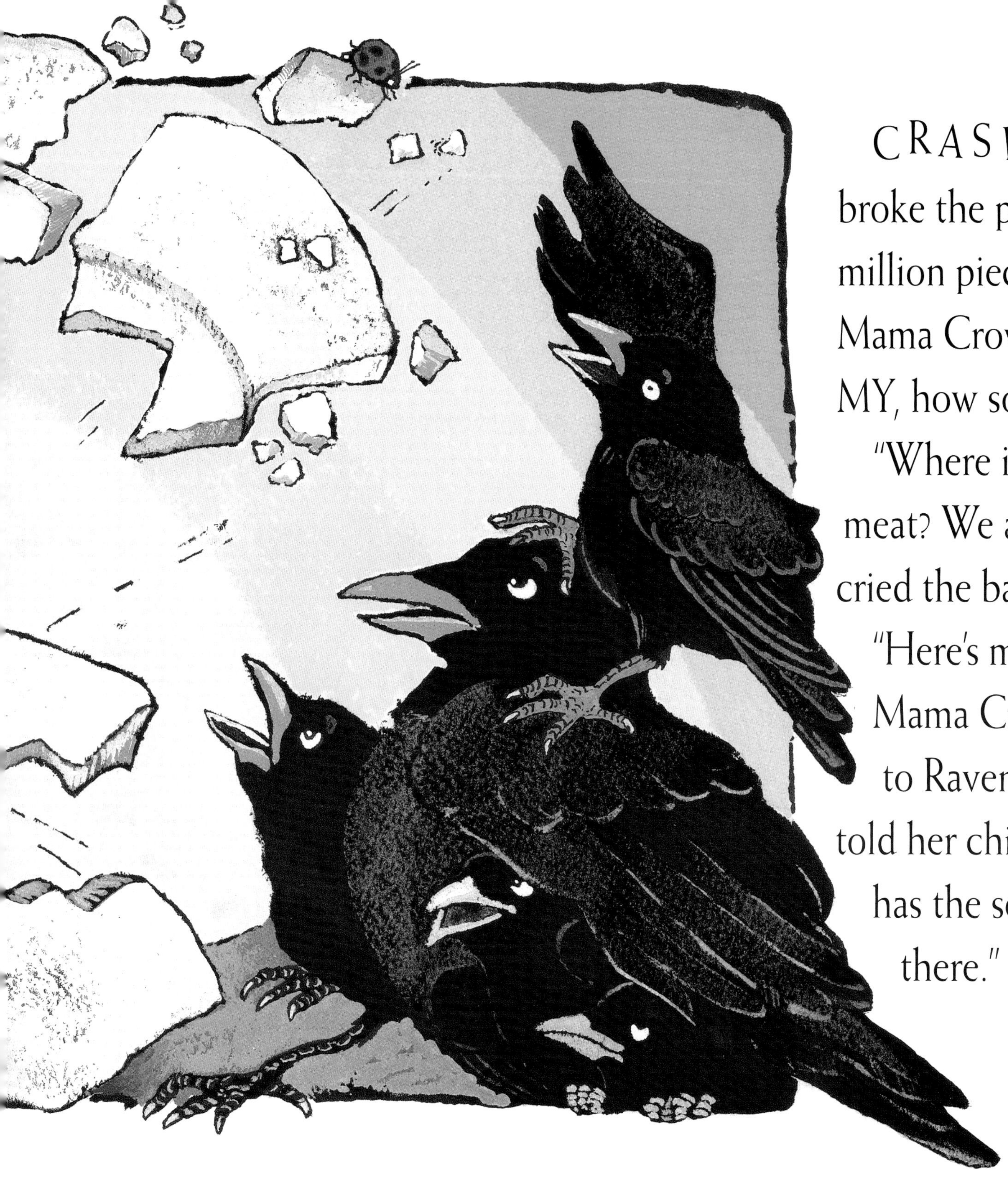

CRASH! The rock broke the platter into a million pieces! Oh, Mama Crow felt bad. MY, how sorry she was.

"Where is the seal meat? We are so *hungry!*" cried the baby crows.

"Here's mischief!" said Mama Crow. "Go over to Raven's house," she told her children. "He has the seal meat there."

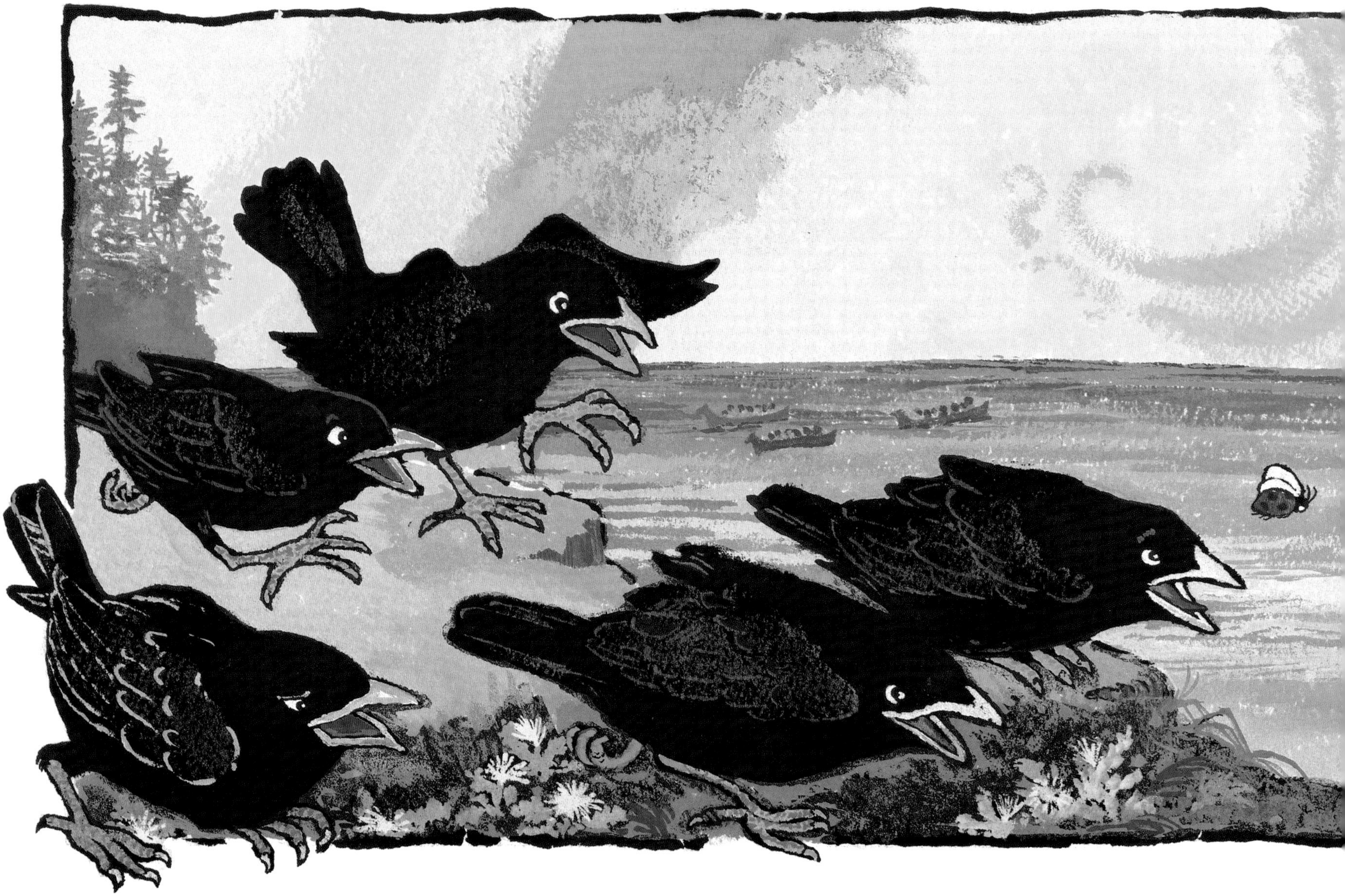

So all the baby crows ran over to Raven's house.

"We're hungry! We're hungry! Where is our seal meat?" cried the baby crows.

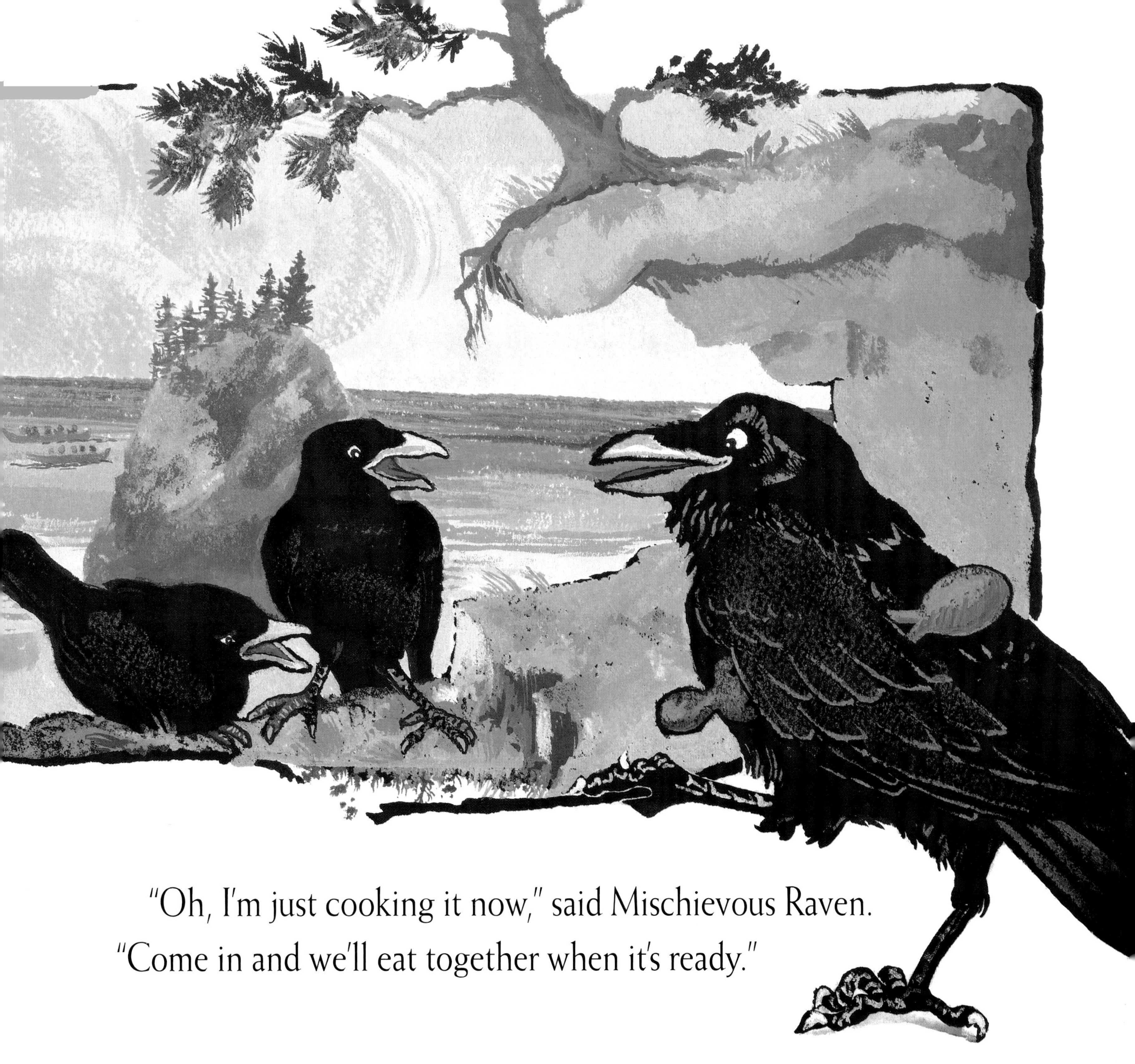

"Oh, I'm just cooking it now," said Mischievous Raven. "Come in and we'll eat together when it's ready."

The baby crows smelled the seal meat cooking. It smelled good. Oh MY, how good it smelled.

Then one baby crow asked, "When is it going to be ready?"

Raven told them, "Oh, just a little while now. Why don't you dance? Before you know it, the seal meat will be ready. Dance now."

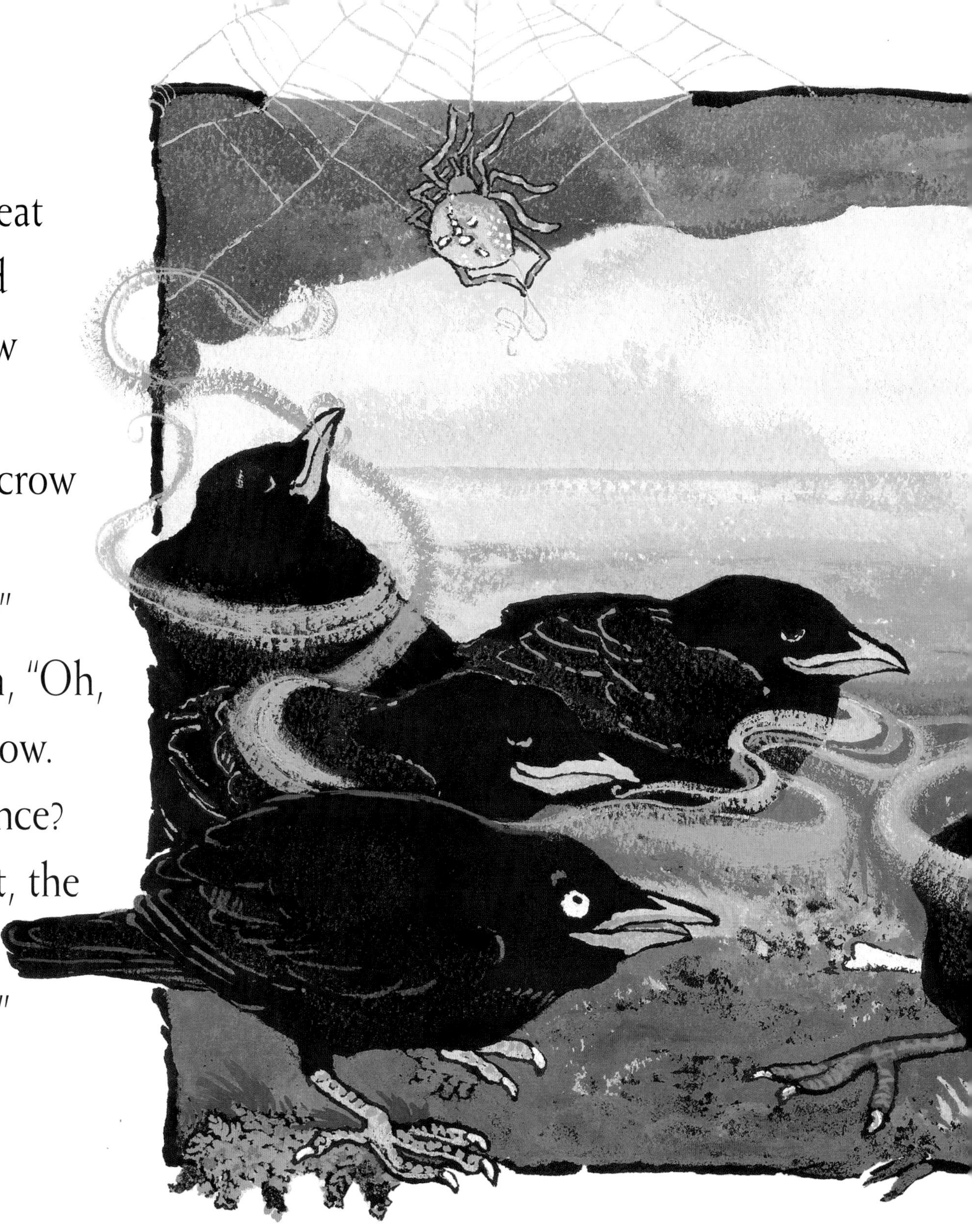

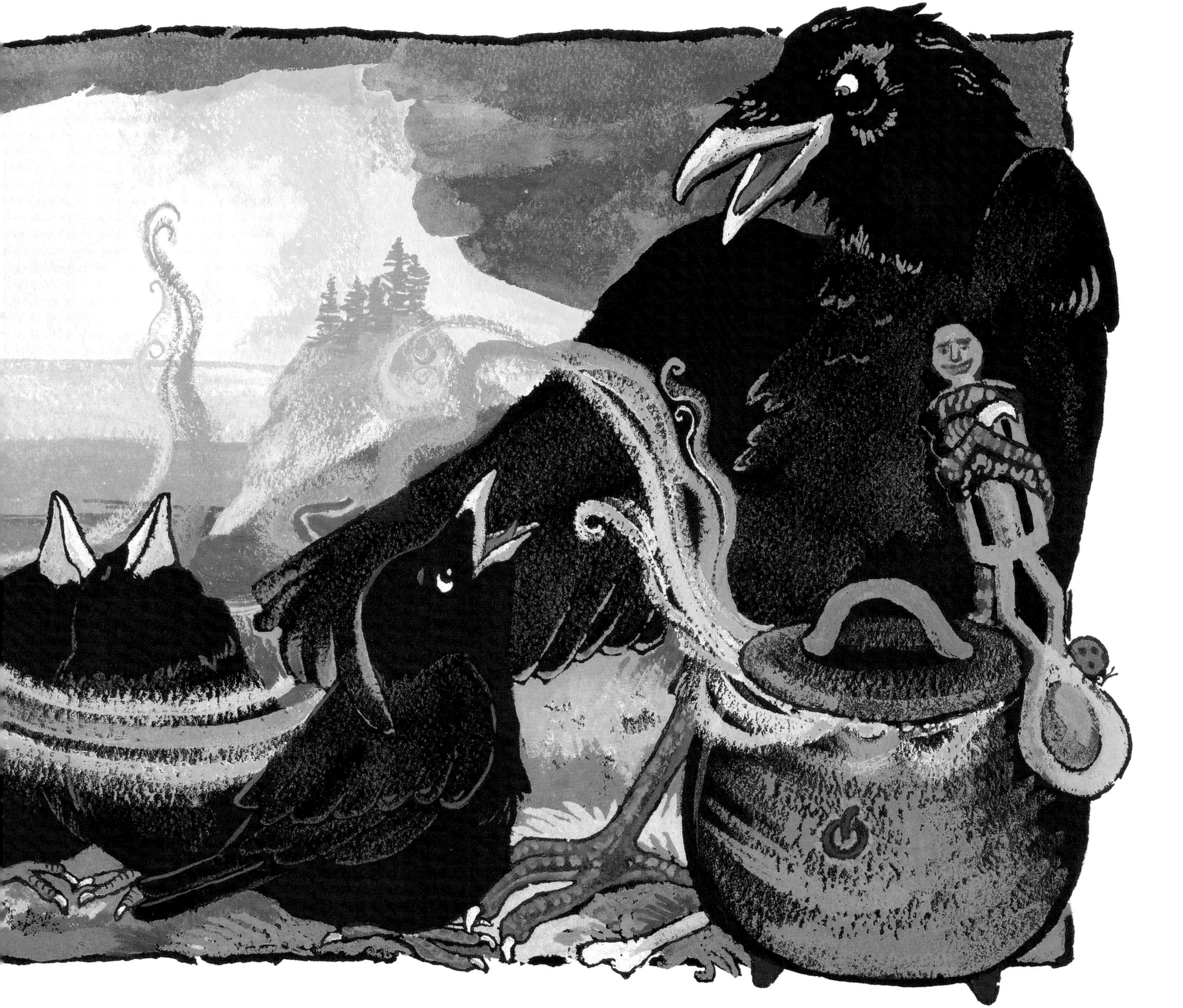

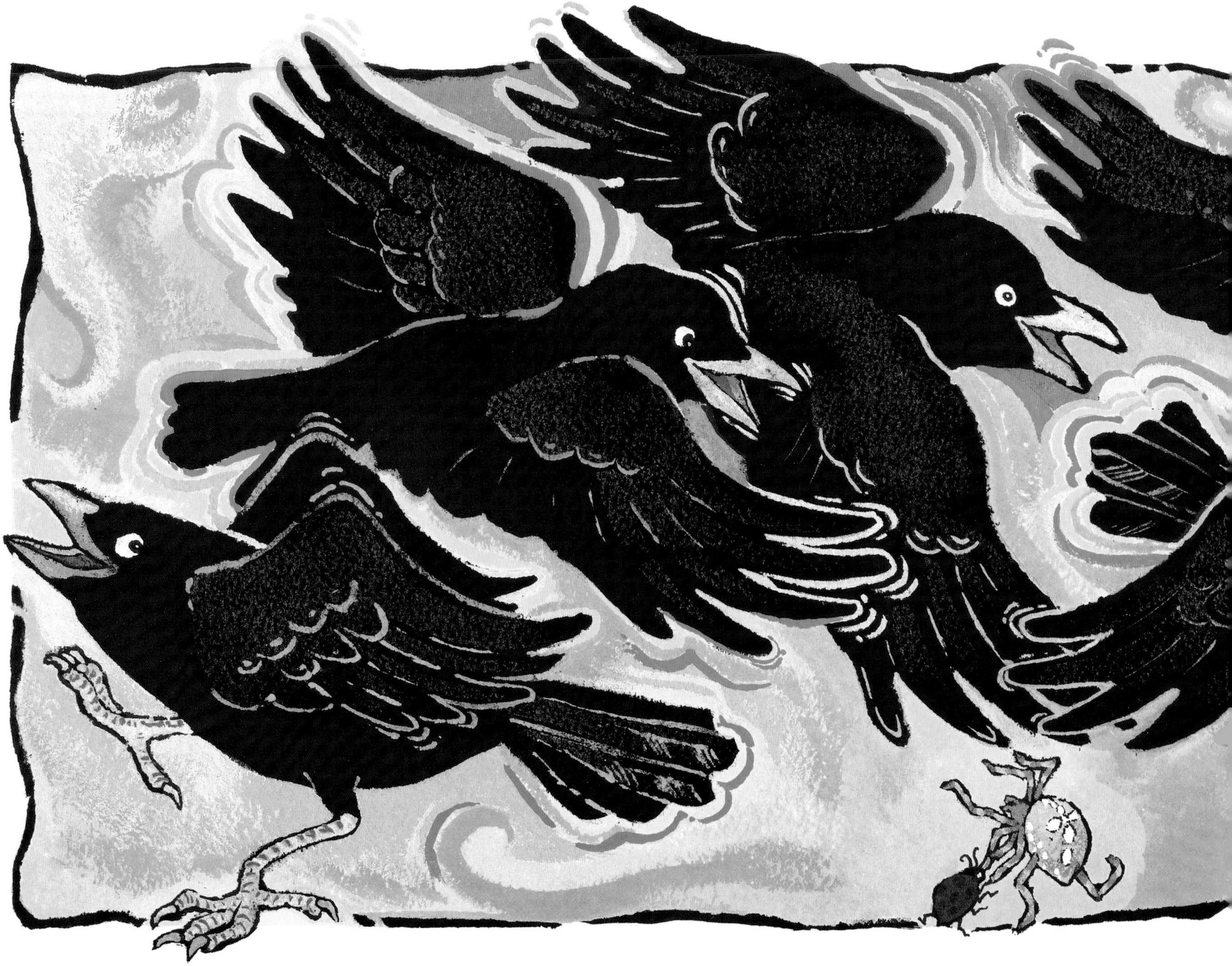

So the baby crows danced and sang and sang and danced.

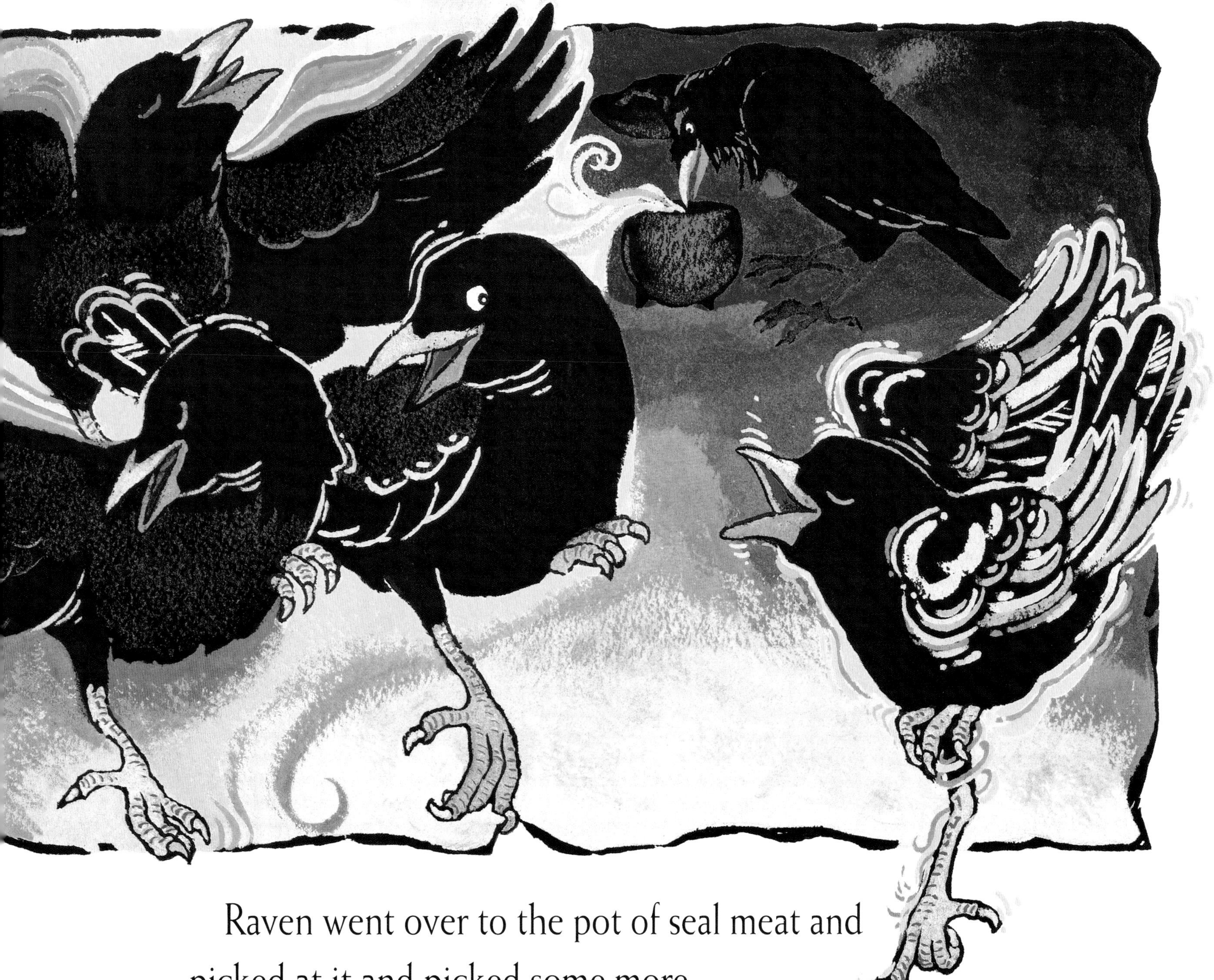

Raven went over to the pot of seal meat and picked at it and picked some more.

The baby crows kept dancing and dancing.

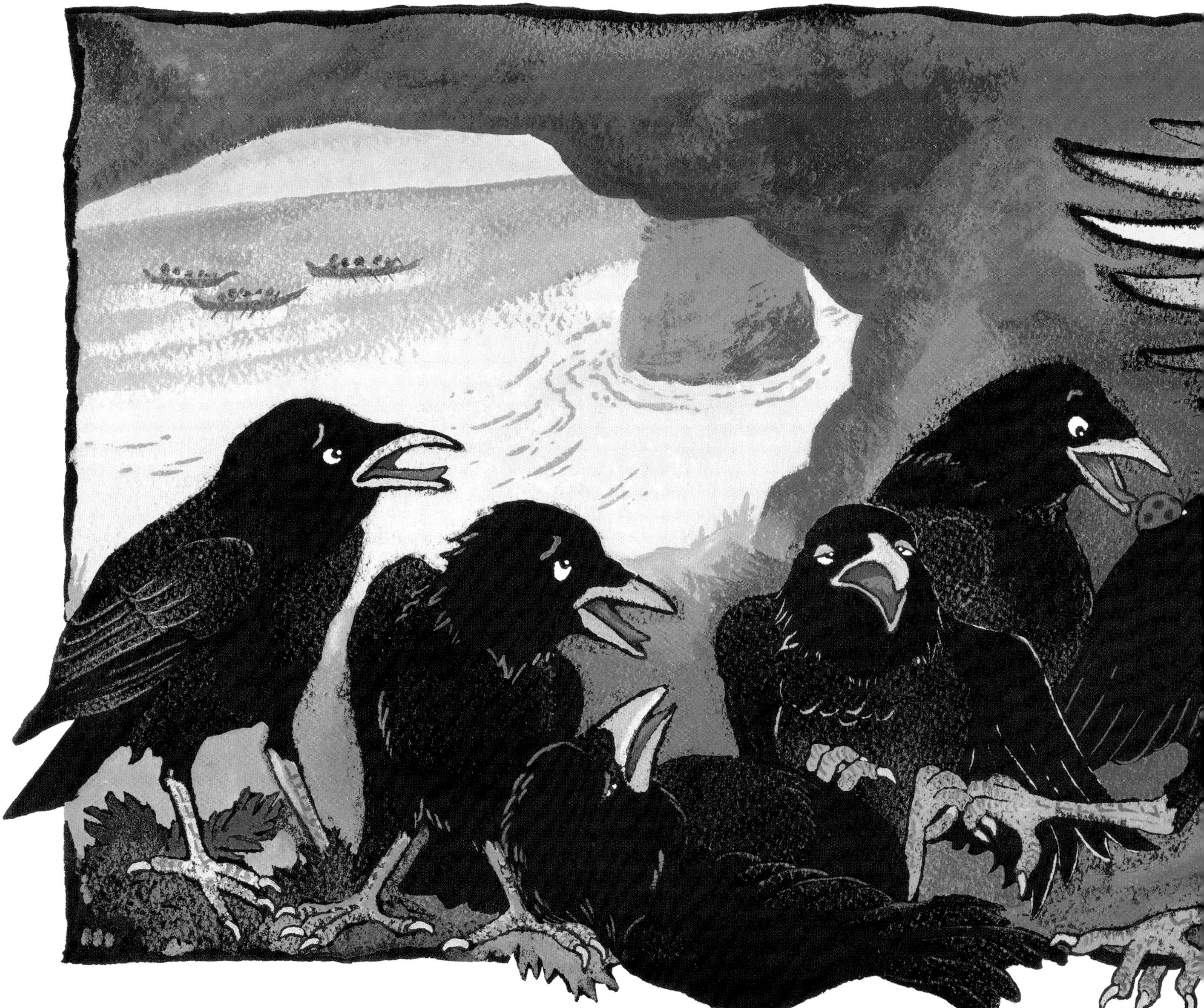

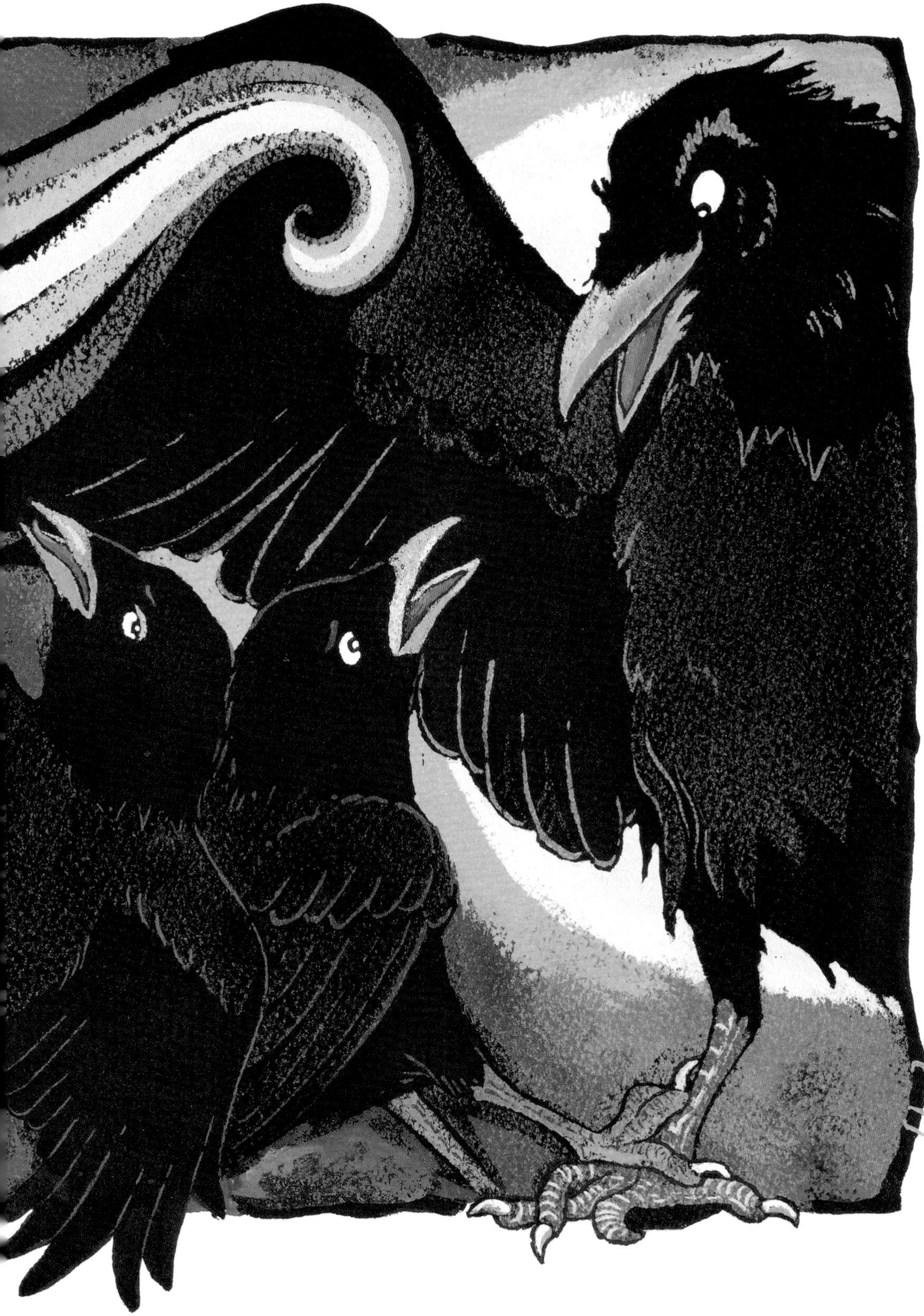

Finally, they grew tired and stopped.

"How much longer is it going to take, Raven? We're tired of dancing. We have been dancing a long time now," said the baby crows.

"Oh, it's ready now," said Mischievous Raven.

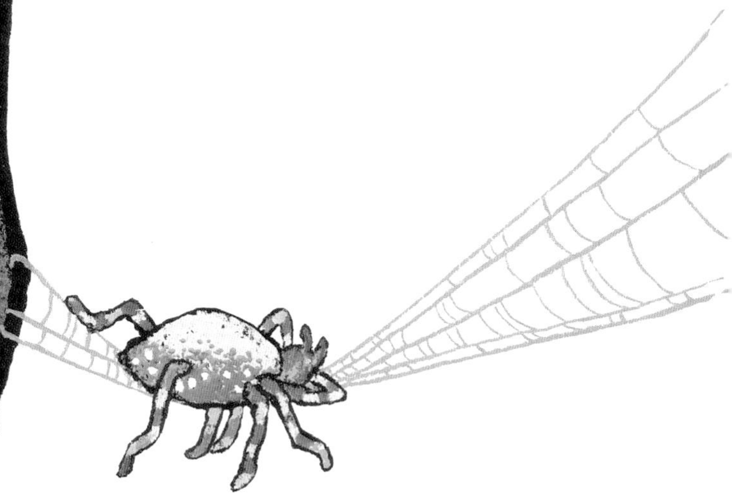

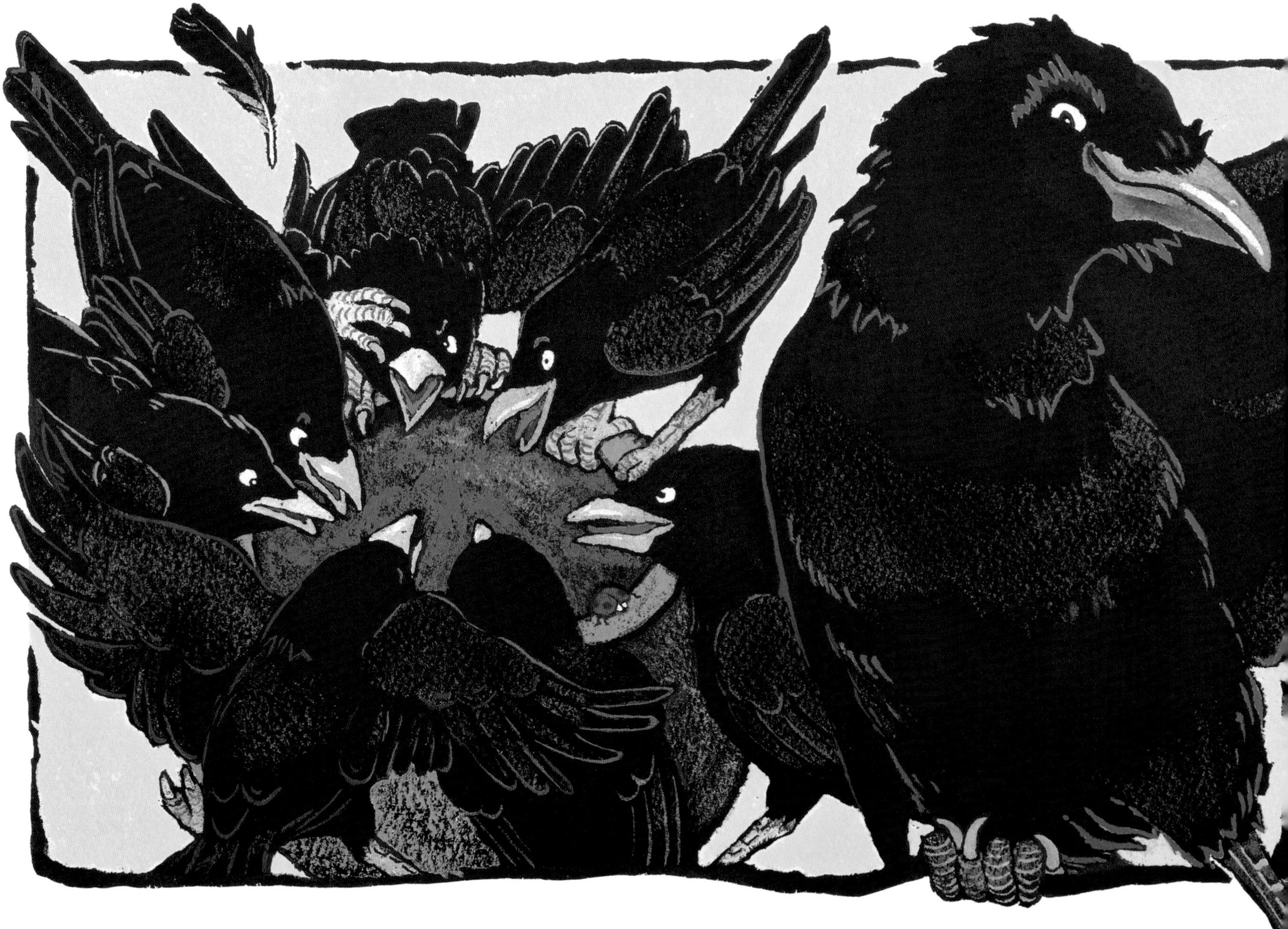

The baby crows were happy. MY, how happy they were! They ran over to the pot, and Raven took off the lid.

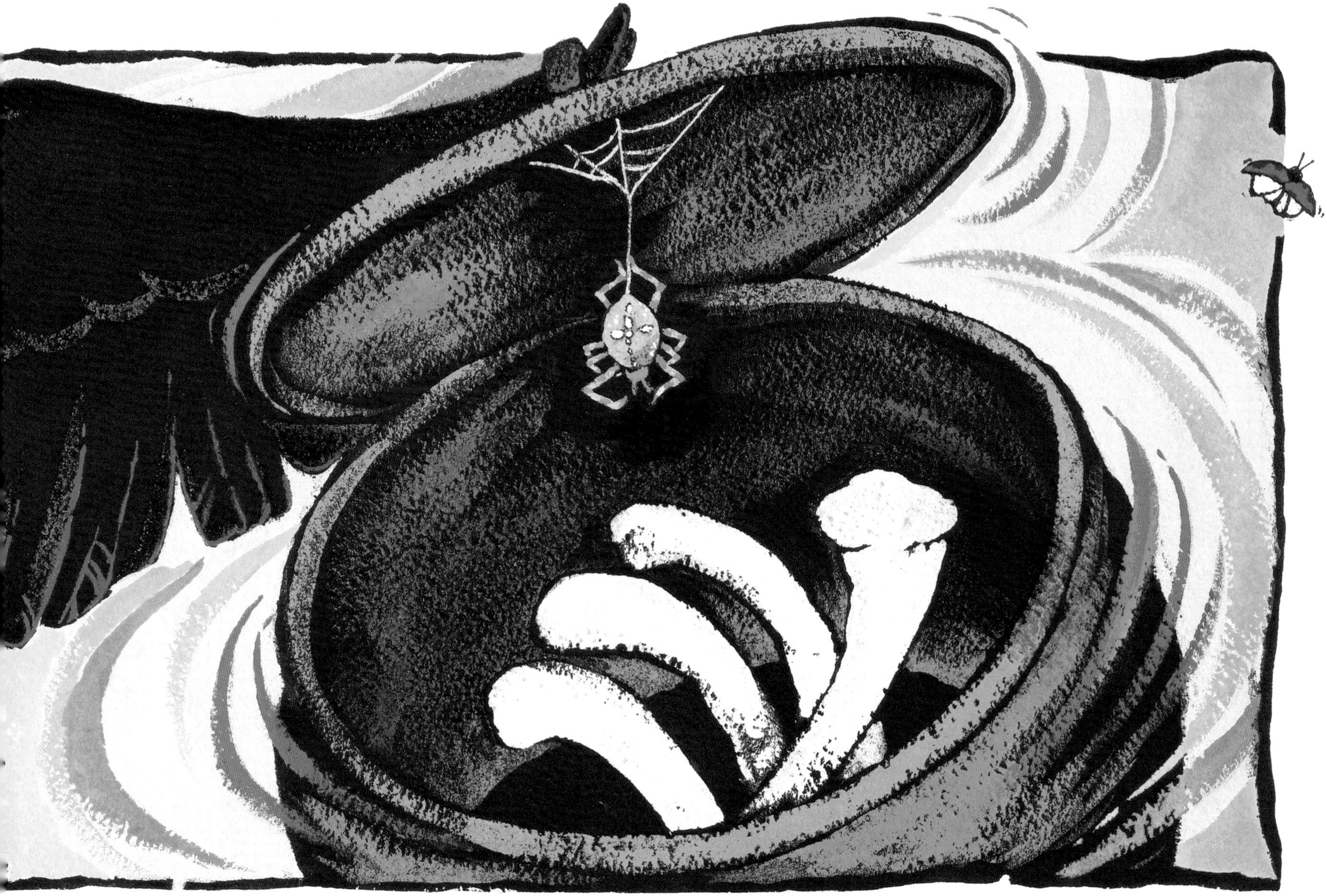

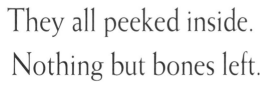

They all peeked inside.
Nothing but bones left.

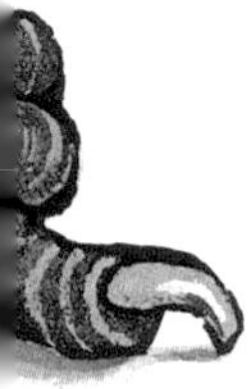

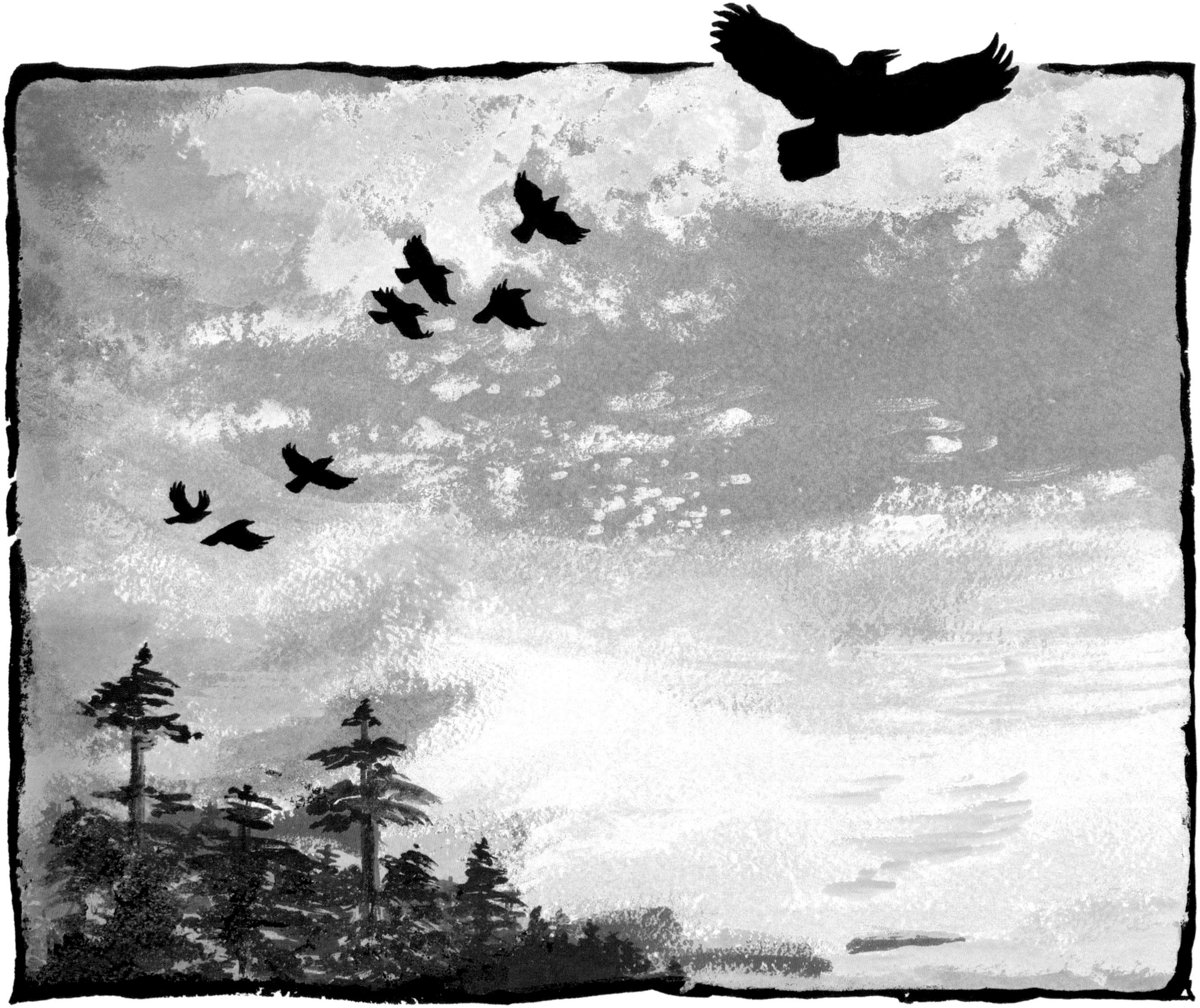

That's all!